RECONSTRUCTION
The Story of Corrie Matthews

By: Ursula L Smith

All scripture quotations labeled KJV are from the King James Version of the Bible.

For copyright purposes, scriptures were unable to be translated, but please feel free to reference any scripture to a version that allows a better understanding for you.

To my beautiful and wonderfully made daughters,

KIERA & KAYLA

For sixteen years I have watched you grow and develop into smart, bold, God-fearing young ladies. You are my happy when I want to feel sad, you are my laughter when life around me isn't funny, but most importantly, you have been my strength throughout my years of growth. From a young mother having no idea what to expect, you trusted me every step of the way, allowing room for mistakes and do-overs. I thank you for your understanding, for your patience and unconditional love for a mother who has not always known the right things to say.

Thank you for walking with me in the darkest places, withstanding all the tough times that brought us to the point we are now. Forced to grow up and become the role model you could look up to and be proud of, you are the reason I fight so hard. May your light continue to shine for everyone to see the love and joy I get to experience every day. You are the change your generation needs, and I am so thankful God trusted me to be your mother, your nurturer, your disciplinarian, and your best friend!

I love you from my whole heart…ALWAYS have and ALWAYS will!

Preface

When I first began writing this book, I was seeking approval from others and my intentions were not the same as God's plans. I desired a much different outcome for Corrie's life, wanting to write and appease to an audience for entertainment purposes only. However, over a year's time, He shifted my direction and way of thinking in order to reach people who needed to know they are not alone in this broken world. Gradually turning into an inspiration, led by the Holy Spirit, with an intent of helping people to understand they were not the only ones to experience trauma, heartache, disappointment, loss, rejection, drug abuse, alcoholism, and abandonment, this book highlights some clear-cut, definitive situations, leaving no room for confusion nor doubts. The intent of this story is to acknowledge that no matter what curve ball life throws your way, there is still hope and our freedom resides in the One who cares for us the most. This world and culture do not define who we are nor what we can become and no matter what you have done in your past, there is still time for you to repent and give your life to Him. For it is in your weakness that His power is perfected.

This book invites you into a world of chaos and from start to finish you will journey through Corrie's life, on some realistic life moments that were intended to destroy who she was born to be. Although she did not make the best decisions, God never gave up on her and He fought for his child to the end. Eager to remain in her family's territory, the enemy did not desire her belongings, just as he does not want any of ours. He seeks to destroy your mind, implanting doubt, hurt, fear, and confusion. Yet, the beauty lies in our discovery of knowing we don't have to remain in that dark place.

Please understand that, in no way am I preaching or attempting to force any source of religion on anyone. You have the right to choose and God gives you that decision to make on your own. However, with all the propaganda and influences of social media and expectations to become someone who we were not destined to become, it is easy to buy into being like everyone else just so we can fit in. So, whatever you chose, make sure it is authentic and not what someone else proposed.

And you hath he quickened, who were dead in trespasses and sins; Wherein in time past ye walked according to the course of this world, according to the prince of the power of the air, the spirit that now worketh in the children of disobedience: Among whom also we all had our conversation in times past in the lusts of our flesh, fulfilling the desires of the flesh and of the mind; and were by nature the children of wrath, even as others. But God, who is rich in mercy, for his great love wherewith He loved us, Even when we were dead in sins, hath quickened us together in heavenly places in Christ Jesus: That in the ages to come He might shew the exceeding riches of His grace in His kindness toward us through Christ Jesus. For by grace are ye saved through faith; and that not of yourselves: it is the gift of God: Not of works, lest any man should boast. For we are His workmanship, created in Christ Jesus unto good works, which God hath before ordained that we should walk in them.

Ephesians 2:1-10 KJV

BOOK ONE

THE DEFINITION OF CORRIE MATTHEWS

Prologue

"These things I have spoken unto you, that in me ye might have peace. In the world ye shall have tribulation: but be of good cheer; I have overcome the world."
John 16:33 KJV

I can honestly admit I have not always looked to the word for advice. As a matter of fact, I am still growing in my faith and in my knowledge of the bible. And since I am being honest, it was tragedy that made me call out to Him, to seek Him, and be still while waiting to feel His presence. In my mind I was thinking all my transgressions and cynical behavior finally caught up with me and I was being punished through constant grief and restraint towards life. I was wrapped up in the world, thinking I was in control and everything that was happening was all because of me, and me alone. What I failed to realize was, there was something bigger than me, larger than anything I could ever imagine, and what they say about faith without work, also applied to work without faith. We are not in control of our own destiny and no matter how hard I tried to test that theory against my own life, I only created a mess. But when I let go and let God… everything began to fall into place.

We are not given the ability to choose our life, to choose our family, or to choose our destination to where it leads us. Gradually learning I am not the controller of my own ship, everything I attempted to avoid hit me like a head on collision. If you can think it, most likely I had been through it. However, rather than being grateful for the battles I had already overcome, I became bitter with the life ahead, feeling like the odds were against me and I must have been one of God's rejects. The question of my existence grew rapidly as peace became just a word that I knew nothing about.

Who knew at such a young age we can be tarnished by life? As if being born into poverty, sexual abuse and molestation were not enough, I slowly fell into depression, no longer having a desire to live and attempting to end it all, but it didn't work out as I planned. You see, God has a way of showing up when we least expect. He never put more on us than we can handle and if we allow Him to lead in every battle, we are guaranteed to win!

Your story is not my story and our lives are not structured the same, but God has a plan for all of us and we were created with a divine purpose. Everything that was meant to destroy me, made me stronger.

Chapter 1

According to statistics, more than sixty percent of U.S households are being ran by single mothers. Also, in the U.S alone, there are hundreds of thousands of children being raised in foster homes. If you did not grow up in one of these categories, you had a head start in life but still, some sort of battle that waits for you ahead. Unfortunately for myself, I was part of both dysfunctions and for years I allowed myself to become disabled by the thoughts that my father did not want me, and my mother was not there. I gravitated to the idea of being a loner and refused to believe I was loved by anyone. And then, if that was not enough, I convinced myself I deserved everything that was coming my way.

Corrie, it's not your fault.

The last memory of my mother was composed of one sentence on a torn piece of what appeared to be a brown paper bag. I was staring silently, taking in every word as though I was encouraging myself to take the high road. Still hung over from the night before, I sought reason and rational for being amongst the living. Wasted nights spent sleeping with random men and taking off my clothes freely seemed to be the "better" my absent, now deceased mother was speaking of. Waking up to a trashed hotel room with condoms all over the floor that morning reassured me that I had played the starring role and was the life of the party the night before, or a whore as others would call me. Although I could barely remember the details, the amount of money I made was all worth it.

"Corrie you're up in five." One of the new dancers yelled from the entrance of the downstairs dressing room. I immediately snapped out of my thoughts. Dressed in my hot pink cat suite and black stiletto heels, I took one more glance in the mirror, folded my letter, placing it back into my makeup bag, and walked to the backstage. With the face of a super model and the physique of a playboy bunny, only apart from having more curves, my body had been my money maker since the young age of fourteen.

Sometimes life presents the toughest obstacles to cause you to open your eyes and look at situations from a different perspective. During this time, it taught me not to care about other opinions. I was not born into a life of riches, no role model to teach me any differently from what I knew. My seventeen years of hustle came straight from the streets. Not believing life had a purpose for me, I became lost and on a path of self-destruction. It was the hustle in me that gave me the drive to do what I was doing; but I loved it. It aroused my curiosities and made me feel all hot and tingly inside.

As the lights began to dim and the music started to play, I could hear DJ Tux announce my arrival to the stage. I stepped from behind the curtain with sass and sex appeal. Working out daily to maintain my physique, my frame stood five feet, seven inches tall with voluptuous legs and thick thighs. My body was toned, curves perfectly sculpted, and my new D cups and Brazilian butt lift sealed the deal every time. My caramel toned skin was smooth and flawless, and my natural, hazel eyes were more than just mesmerizing. I knew I was the "sugar, honey, iced tea" and so did everyone else.

In a dark room with one bright light flashing in my face, I saw nothing. As I became more visible to the audience, I began to hear whistles while Trilogy's Wicked Games played loudly over the speakers throughout the club. The two Xanax bars and small bottle of vodka I consumed thirty minutes prior was finally taking hold of my body, causing me to feel completely relaxed. I began to move seductively to the music, caressing my body as if I was the only one in the room. Left to right, I rocked slowly. And as aroused as I was trying to make my audience, I was already there, taking myself to the next level while preparing for what was going to take place once the song stopped and my shift ended.

Chapter 2

A loss of identity can leave you feeling empty with no purpose. Often, we are just wandering through life in hopes of getting it right the first time. But how is this possible when we have no clue where to begin? We continue to make the same mistakes, gambling with the most precious possession that could ever be gifted to us.

When people would ask, I would tell them my childhood was anything but normal, that I practically raised myself, and nobody cared. But now I know that is far from the truth because God cared. Blinded by what the enemy wanted me to see, I allowed him in my territory, clouding my vision of truth. My mother worked to provide for two kids and made the sacrifices necessary for all to survive. Looking back, I recognize the struggle and the hardship, but I now understand her strength and independence. She was everything God meant for her to be in my life at that time and He made no mistakes.

For you to understand my circumstance, you would first have to know my struggle with growing up as a child. I saw a lot, and I experienced more than you could imagine. But I was not alone. God calls children a blessing and a gift, filled with innocence, laughter, and joy. But what about when that innocence is stripped away?

Train up a child in the way he should go and when he is old, he will not depart from it.

Proverbs 22:6 KJV

Twenty-One Years Previous....

"Corrie, I'm not going to tell you again to get up." My mom was yelling through the house, becoming angrier at my defiance. I laid on my worn, twin size mattress, wide awake for what seemed like hours. Contemplating how I could fake sick; I did not want to go to school.

We just moved to my grandparents' house, or what was left of it anyway and once again, I was sharing a room with my mother while my brother got the luxury of having his own space. The house was quite old. Built of worn, rotted wood, the floors were squeaky, and there was little to no insulation. It was freezing cold in the winters and depressingly hot during the summers. We used a nail on the front door for a knob and whenever you would walk in the bathroom it felt as though you were guaranteed to fall right through the floors. Rodents crept through the walls at night, as an indicator we were not living alone. But as mama would say, "it's a roof". Not wanting to leave my old neighborhood and all my friends, I desired more than anything to move back, but mama could no longer deal with the antics of the landlord popping up, requesting sexual favors in exchange for rent money he knew she did not have.

My brother was still tucked away in bed, sound asleep, and mama was scrambling to make it on time to work. "Edna will be here in five minutes to take you to school and you better be ready." She yelled at me once more as she rushed out the door, slamming it behind her. The loud "bam" sound was sure to wake everyone in the neighborhood. She was a very small, petite woman who worked two jobs at a time to provide for two kids on her own, working as many hours as time would allow. My older brother, Jamal, was my care giver and often did a messed-up job at it. Locked out on several occasions, I began roaming the streets at a very young age. My childhood had been anything but normal, quickly learning this world was colder than Antarctica in July of 1983.

Hurrying to the bathroom, I glanced to my right at the bedroom door leading to the room my uncle had been utilizing all twenty-six years of his life. He was the youngest of three, my mom being the oldest. But since he was mentally challenged, he refused to live anywhere other than the house he grew up in. He kept to himself and was very possessive over the little belongings he did have. My mom called it a "homeless person syndrome", but the weird part was, he had never been homeless. Up until six months prior, all their lives took a turn for the worse after my grandparents had passed. Uncle Blu became very dependent on prescription drugs in addition to the one's he had already been on for his disability. Uncle Joe, the middle son, was incarcerated for trying to rob a convenient store for a carton of cigarettes. Left to maintain the house along with all the bills and my uncle, my mother became discouraged and all hope was lost. Although I was too young to understand how it truly affected the day to day progress of life, I watched as the silent killer called depression began to eat away at her.

Entering the bathroom, I quickly brushed my teeth and washed my face. Disregarding lotion for my ashy skin, I put on my denim jeans and plaid button-down shirt, finishing it off with my tattered tennis shoes handed down to me by a neighbor. My hair was straight from the chemicals my mother applied to it days earlier, but since I did not know of any other styles, it was often pulled back into a ponytail.

Grabbing my clear see-through backpack, I made it outside just as Ms. Edna was pulling up in her old, 1978 Oldsmobile Cutlass. The paint was peeling, and the seats were dirty and worn. If you were to raise the floor mats you could look down out of a rusty hole to see the highway. The engine running hot, smoked profusely; which explained the jug of water she often carried. And whenever she would come to a stop, the brakes screeched and scrubbed for their lives.

I ran to the car and hopped in the back seat with the other four kids that were already squeezed in tightly. Placing my backpack in my lap, I closed the door as we pulled off. With the school only being blocks away, we arrived within minutes. "Thank you, Ms. Edna,", rushing out of the car and leaving the others behind before any of my friends were to see me. Although grateful for the ride, I was too embarrassed by the condition of the car.

Nowadays, television and social media makes it easier for us to get caught up in worldly possessions, wanting to be better than the next, and neglecting to acknowledge the blessings sitting in front of our face. I desired the lavish life that was constantly being presented before me and I sought out to accomplish just that, eager to get out of the poverty-filled life I was born into.

After school, I waited to walk home with the other kids from the neighborhood. It was our daily routine; ride with Ms. Edna in the mornings and walk home in the afternoons. After all, we did not live far. Often in large groups, we would cut through the woods in the backfield of the school and walk through the neighborhood of middle-class families, first arriving at Ms. Edna house where her three girls and two sons lived. Only a block down, the next house would be mine, but I never went there. Instead, I continued around the corner with my friend Lisa and her twin brother Levi. Knowing he had a crush on me, I enjoyed the flirtatious attention and saw nothing wrong with the vulgar comments, often filling me up as we continued down the street to their house.

At the age of ten, I knew more about sex than others had ever expected. Exposed to more than my eyes could handle and my mind could block out, I became experimental with my body, testing my limits and allowing others to take advantage of my vulnerabilities. I craved attention and since my mother was never available to provide it, I sought out to find it in all the wrong places.

Once arriving to Lisa's house, we bypassed going inside and instead found ourselves in a wooded, secluded area in which we were all very familiar with. Using my backpack as a pillow, I placed it on the ground as I proceeded to lay down in the leaves on my back, allowing for Levi to hunch on top of me like a horny jack rabbit, eager to catch the sensations of an orgasm. For what seemed like hours, I closed my eyes to allow myself to go into a place of darkness. In my young, adolescent mind, it was normal for these types of things to happen in low income, poverty filled neighborhoods. Forced to grow up at a very early age, I immediately adapted to my surroundings, not caring about anyone else's opinions of my actions.

Although it never gave me any satisfaction, this took place throughout the school year, eventually growing into what seemed like the entire neighborhood of boys. They would each stand patiently waiting their turn as Lisa silently watched. And though no clothes were ever removed, I was still considered as the girl who had sex with the entire neighborhood of boys. A neighborhood tramp still in elementary school, lost, confused, and completely out of my league. Who was I? More importantly, who was I becoming?

Having no regard for life, I lived recklessly. I knew what to expect daily and I was comfortable with it. Never did it cross my mind to consider what my mother would say if she knew what her daughter was out here in these streets doing nor did I care about how she would feel. I was living my life the way I though it should be, breaking every rule as I would go. Within those years, I became an accomplice of stealing, although I had not gotten caught, and even subjected myself to twerking and popping for the older teenage boys, sometimes exposing my genitals to make it more realistic.

It did not take long for my mother to catch wind of the situation. Everyone in the neighborhood was talking, eventually getting back to Jamal. She yelled and screamed, expressing to me how disgusting I was and how I would never amount to much. I was stupid, a tramp, even the B word; everything but her little girl. Feeling heavily condemned by my so-called loved ones and convinced I was the only daughter who was subdued by a mother's words of obvious disappointment, I hated life but most of all, I hated the family I was forced to live with. Never at home, in my mind she had no right to tell me how to act. Leaving me in the hands of my teenage brother, she never took the time to nurture me and teach me how a young lady should carry herself. The only thing she showed me was how to depend on different men, allowing for them to use and abuse her before moving on to the next. Often looking for love in all the wrong places, she was lost and reckless, a pattern I quickly adapted to becoming a part of. I was falling victim to her mistakes and playing the role was natural. Never did I realize the consequences of my actions until my actions became my consequences.

Open thou mine eyes, that I may behold wondrous things out of thy law.

Psalms 119:18 KJV

As time rolled on, life for me began to become even darker. At the age of eighteen, Jamal's life was tragically taken and for the first time I experienced loss like no other. He was my caregiver, my best friend, and the only one who made time for me. His funeral was depressing, and I cried like I never cried before. My heart was hurting so badly, and I lacked understanding. With no one to comfort me, I was left to heal alone, my mom grieving in her own way as well. In my house, counseling was not an option.

Rapidly, my mother fell into a deeper depression, allowing grief to consume her, depending on daily medications from the streets to keep her calm. Nothing was the same and she never understood how life could continue. Her heart was broken, unable to pick up the pieces to move on and the only resolution was laying in her bed, crying the pain away. Days turned into weeks and weeks into months with no light at the end of her tunnel. She never returned to work, causing all the bills to fall behind. With no food to eat and most utilities being cut off, she was heartbroken and helpless to her circumstances.

One night, as I laid in my bed, a strong feeling something was wrong came to me. Mama paced down the hallway for hours, crying and sobbing hysterically. And suddenly, there was a dead silence. It was so quiet I could hear the critters as they made their way throughout the walls. I could no longer hear footsteps from her walking back and forth, and the crying ceased. For a moment, I laid thinking she had fallen asleep in another room. But as time passed, I decided to go see if maybe she left. I was terrified of what I found. Ingesting a full prescription of pills, my mother's lifeless body laid in the bathtub, leaving me all alone to fend for myself. Four months from burying my brother, I was forced to say goodbye to her as well. At only the young age of thirty-eight, she decided to give up the fight and surrender to the lies of the enemy. I was turned over to social services, bouncing around from foster home to foster home and the only thing I had left was the letter she wrote moments before.

Chapter 3

We are physically created by our mothers and fathers but that does not mean our identity is defined by these specific beings. Must we forget they were also created and chosen by the same creator who created us? Our purpose has already been established by Him, yet the lies of the enemy want us to believe differently. We are not our parents' mistakes. We do not have to carry the burdens of their transgressions. The one who meditates on the hand they have been dealt, rather than maneuvering their way through the wilderness with Jesus, will never make it out of that destructive territory. Paint a bigger picture, one of newness and built solid on faith and faith alone.

Most my summers, for years, were isolated. Ripped away from my southern roots, I was eventually forced to live up north with my father who moved two years prior to my mother's suicide. Somehow the state managed to contact him after I had given so many families trouble. But little did I know, that would not be the last move for me. Breaking curfew, going to jail on minor marijuana charges, drinking myself nearly into a comma, and let's not forget getting pregnant, gave my dad plenty enough assurance to want nothing to do with me once I graduated high school. I was exposed to more up north than I could have ever imagined down south. He was clueless to the responsibility he had taken on, having to raise a rebellious thirteen-year-old, and could not wait to be rid of me. Rather than completing my four years of high school, I dropped out and opted for my GED instead. My dad offered to buy me a one-way ticket to anywhere I choose to go, giving me some money for the ride along the way.

Not even twenty minutes into my eighteenth birthday, I was starting a new life back down south and away from everything I had grown to love for five years. I decided to bypass my country roots of Alabama and go straight to Florida. Sitting patiently by the window, starring out at the highway as the bus merged onto the New Jersey Turnpike, tears rolled down my face uncontrollably from all the mixed emotions. My father no longer possessed the patience to care for me and I had no other family. Not yet ready to give up my adopted lifestyle, I was stepping outside of my comfort zone, beginning life as an adult but alone and feeling like an outcast.

Growing even more impatient, I stood up, stretching my legs before making my way to the bathroom. As I opened the door, I inhaled the disgusting smell of urine mixed with air freshener which filled the small, confined space. I took a quick glance at myself in the mirror, touching up the strands of hair that had become dismembered from the rest of my long, silky ponytail before reaching into my pocket to pull out a small bottle of Xanax pills. After popping one in my mouth I walked back to my seat, not realizing we had come to another stop. With a little hesitation, I decided to step off for a moment to catch some fresh air.

Even as early as 11:35 in the morning, the weather was at a high temperature of eighty-one with no chance of cooling off. In the east, this was considered hot, but I heard it was worse down south. The wind was blowing very lightly and there was no sight of a cloud anywhere in the sky. I quickly located the most secluded area I could find, but not too far so I could keep my eye on the bus.

"Traveling alone?" An unknown gentleman approached me from behind. "I'm a big girl", I mumbled without giving him the benefit of making eye contact. Although I was only a teenager, my experience with life made me aware of the world we lived in. I was far from a rookie when it came to two things… men and sex.

Turning around, I noticed the tall, older man standing there dressed in some blue jeans and a nice silk, button down shirt. He stood approximately five feet eleven inches with a slender figure. His hair was brown with a hint of gray and his eyes were hazel like mine. Although my type of guy would have been much younger and thuggish looking, my curiosity entertained the idea. Surely, I could not have been his ideal type of woman, or girl if you must be technical.

"Where are you headed?"

Not wanting to make my nervousness obvious, "Tampa, Florida", I quickly replied. There was something about him causing me to feel at an unease. I turned to walk back towards the bus but was stopped by the grab of my hand before he seductively pulled me towards him. Nervous and aroused at the same time, I stood in silence. My body pressed against his as he whispered, "how much?"

"Excuse you! Do I look like a prostitute?" My top lip curled, displaying a look of disgust as beads of sweat began to form. Trying to play the innocent role as if I did not know what he was talking about; I was more familiar with the situation than I was willing to allow for him to see. Apparently, his mind was already set on what he wanted and was going to get it at any cost. He reached in his pocket, pulling out his wallet and handing me a one-hundred-dollar bill. "It is yours and I'll give you more once you have fulfilled your obligations to me."

"Are you a cop?" I asked him, feeling like this was a set up and there were going to be several undercover cars pulling up to arrest me once I accepted the offer, but he did not answer. It was clear I was not dealing with a rookie. Taking my chances and considering I would need more money eventually, I reached out to grab it. As he turned to walk towards one of the restrooms, I waited until there was a large amount of distance between us before I began to follow. Nervously approaching the door, I turned the handle to enter, standing in front of a half-naked man. I could feel the nervousness beginning to bubble in my gut, but it was much too late to turn back, and I needed the money.

"I only have five minutes, so we have to make this quick."

"Oh, I plan to", he replied with a smirk on his face. I dropped to my knees and began to please him like only I knew how, never considering him being a stranger, nor of any diseases he may have possessed. At that stage of my life, money dictated my actions. Once it was over, he leaned back on the wall with his pants still down to his ankles, taking a deep breath before exhaling. Not saying a word, I knew my job was done and he was satisfied. Reaching for his pants to give me the rest of the money as promised, nothing else needed to be said. I looked down at the other hundred-dollar bill he handed me before stuffing it in my pocket and exiting the restroom, hurriedly to not be seen.

Once back on the bus, I sat patiently by the window starring out at the highway, at the many trees, and all the sporadic cities we drove through, realizing the growing opportunities for me were endless. I made two hundred dollars in less than fifteen minutes. That was the moment I thought I understood what the rest of my life would be like. Little did I know, life already made plans for me as well.

Chapter 4

__And Joshua saved Rahab the harlot alive, and her father's household, and all that she had; and she dwelleth in Israel even unto this day; because she hid the messengers, which Joshua sent to spy on Jericho.__

__Joshua 6:25 KJV__

Throughout my thirteen years in Tampa, I became quite the entertainer, twerking and spreading my legs were the two things to get me the most money in the smallest amount of time. Starting out as only a temporary fix to my financial problems, I became addicted to the tax-free funds. Though it may sound absurd to many, I refused to subject myself to a regular nine to five, barely making any money once Uncle Sam got his cut. Not to mention, I made my own schedule. Life for me was not checkers, it was chess…. checkmate!

Once arriving in the city of Tampa, I began my journey at the New Beginnings Women and Children Shelter, arranged by my social worker from back home. With only three hundred dollars in my pocket, I searched for work and enrolled in a massage therapy school to learn how to make money working in someone's spa. Plans to be more and have more than I could ever imagine, I wanted money, and I wanted it fast. The women in the shelter were much older, assuming they possessed some sort of experience in hard living. They could point me in the right direction to opportunities, looking like life had served them a pile of crap as well, yet thankful to have made the last call before the doors locked for the night.

To accommodate for my empty pockets, I decided to give amateur night in one of the local clubs a try. One of the cook's from NBWCS introduced the idea and I quickly accepted once she mentioned the payout of five hundred dollars to the first-place winner. Unexpectedly, I walked out with a job and the money. I was paid all cash. The youngest dancer in the club, I worked more hours because I was always requested; becoming more of a full-time dancer, and less of a student to become a massage therapist, convincing myself I was right where I belonged and how fortunate I was to make so much money at my age.

Months from turning nineteen and less than a year invested into the club, I pretty much ran everything and quickly became the princess of Duchess, the top money maker, the 'do anything in the private room as long as you are paying' girl. There were no boundaries and I even had my favorites.

That was the same year I met Nicholas, Nick as I would begin to call him. Born in New Orleans and moving to Tampa to escape the devastation of Katrina, he possessed the cocky swag that drove me to my highest climax. Six years my senior, we met at the club one night while he was out with some friends for a bachelor party. Insisting on getting me alone, I took him to one of the private rooms for a dance. But instead, he paid me for conversation, which lasted for hours. I must have made at least five hundred dollars off him, yet, he never laid a hand on me. He told me he was a businessman, knowing what that meant, even with the minimal details he gave. He was very egotistical but displayed sincerity in his boastfulness. We exchanged numbers and kept in touch daily. Very often he would show up at the club just to see me and soon we began a relationship outside of Duchess, unable to get enough of him as our relationship flourished into more than I could admit to. Moving me out of my trashy, studio apartment complex, he put me in my first, upscale condo with his drug money. Young, gullible, and blinded by what I identified as love, I did whatever, whenever for him, knowing he was never any good for me, even before finding out he was married.

After being arrested, I realized the extent of his hustle and how risky it would be for me to become invested. Of course, I bailed him out one last time with anticipations of letting go of what we had but the breakup never happened. Instead, he spent the night as if my home was his home, my bed was his bed, and I was forever his woman. I did not care that he had a family at home. All I thought about was self, remaining focused and never looking back in order to reach the top. I persuaded him to sell more as he attempted to persuade me to dance less. We were one another's support system and I was always there to bail him out when he got busted.

Thus, were they defiled with their own works, and went a whoring with their own inventions.

Psalms 106:39 KJV

A year later, I began a different role outside of dancing in the club and sex for me became more of a hobby rather than for pleasure. Only difference was, I mad an extremely large amount of money in a very creative way. I eventually finished school and obtained my state license to practice massage therapy. However, massages were not the only things being offered.

Buried into work, day after day, night after night, I scheduled regulars often, rarely having any room for walk-in's due to the need of continuing my commitment at the club. I made a great bit of money doing both, but never allowing clients to my house.

In the back of the spa was a very intimate themed setup which allowed for me to entertain men who were in high positions, such as judges and commissioners. I was running a whore house within a legal institute with no intentions of being caught. Learning from the best, Nick was my inspiration in Hustle 101. He grew to hate how I made my money but we both agreed not to speak on neither's occupation. As degrading as mine may have seemed, he jeopardized serving serious time as well and was no longer providing the income. It was time for him to step aside and let me show him I could run a legitimate, illegal business. Besides, Nick had not been my first encounter with a drug dealer. Already "hot in the pants" as my mother would always say, by the time I was fifteen, my curiosities had grown beyond the thoughts of someone in my age bracket.

Chapter 5

My outlook on life stemmed from the negative cycles of my upbringing, while not having a positive role model left me open for exploring life on my own. Eager to escape the rotation of my tragedies and disappointments, I now understand why the root of my focus became money, greed, and selfishness.

Thinking back on summer of nineteen ninety-six, listening to artist such as 2Pac, Ice Cube, Snoop Dog, and hanging with the guys in the neighborhood were things of the norm to me. Never the tomboyish type, I always seemed to get along with guys much easier than females and I was very well-known around the block. At fifteen, I became more curious about the idea of having sex, having my picks and chooses of the guys I would let dry hump me just for the fun of it. In my mind, it was not a big deal because there was never any penetration, so I was still able to hold my status as a virgin.

I can remember one day, while walking home from the corner store, a brand-new Mercedes pulled up beside me. I was wearing some tight, fitted jeans and a sky-blue halter top. My hair was pressed straight, and I wore sunglasses to protect my eyes from the sun. Always curvy with a slender waist, adult men use to hit on me because they thought I was older, so it was of no surprise when the man in the driver seat rolled down his window and began to stare. Treating him no differently, I continued to walk nonchalantly as he gradually drove to my speed.

"Excuse me beautiful, can I holla at you for a sec?"

To me it was only another lame line with no purpose. It was obvious from his kitted out, overpriced car that he was a drug dealer preying on anything that would give him the time of day. Instead, I continued to ignore him. Continuing to walk on the sidewalk for what seemed like miles, he continued to follow in his truck like a lost puppy for two more blocks before deciding to park and get out. He was wearing some grey sweatpants with a white t-shirt and some all-white Adidas. And as he began to approach me, I stared at his masculine body, his numerous tattoos and then at his soft lips. My mind was taking me places a girl my age should never be able to imagine. And when he opened his mouth to speak it was like my entire body was talking back.

"What's up? Where you headed beautiful?"

"Home."

While attempting to seem mature and confident I told him I was eighteen. Mentally and physically I felt like I was there, but the reality remained that I was way too young to entertain a conversation with a grown man. 5'10, light skinned complexion, Justin was everything I was not interested in, yet, charming enough to grab my attention. The definition of his muscles rippled from his waste up and tattoos covered his entire body from what I could see. His pearly white teeth could light up an entire room whenever he smiled, and his dimples made it much harder to look away. He was twenty-three at the time and there was no way he would have ever given me a second glance had he known I was young enough to send him straight to jail.

For days, we hung out nonstop, becoming inseparable the entire summer. He took me around the city, showing me places I never seen and before long, my immature, simple mind allowed me to become mesmerized by his actions. I wanted to be with him nonstop, every hour, every minute, every second. What should have been puppy love for someone my age became something much more with him. Still not knowing about the eight-year age difference, he treated me like a woman, as my mind continued to be manipulated by the enemy. Not knowing any better, I sought truth in my actions, with a need to belong. And although he never called me his girlfriend, I expected we were much more than just friends; proven on a Sunday night when Justin picked me up from my house a little after seven.

"Is that Justin's car out front?" My stepmother Dana looked infuriated at the thought of the neighborhood drug dealer picking up the family ingrate. My dad worked over-night, leaving once I arrived home in the afternoons. Desperate to obtain a role in my life, Dana attempted to carry herself more as a mother figure but soon realized she could never control my rooted ways. My heart remained closed to the idea of her trying to play a parent when it seemed most convenient.

"I don't need your validation. It's not a big deal anyway."

Dana gave me a look of disappointment but said nothing else about the matter, knowing she soon would be rid of me. Months away from turning sixteen and growing more rebellious, it was going to take a lot more hits from life to slow me down, believing survival was all on me.

I calmly walked out of the front door, not wanting Justin to see me upset and asking questions. I was wearing an all-black baby doll dress with some embellished, crisscross sandals, nothing too fancy in my attempt to seem mature. With a smile, he greeted me as I walked over to the passenger side door and got into the truck, anxious to see what the night was going to bring. Butterflies fluttered in my stomach and my palms began to sweat. Justin always presented himself as laid back, never too much to say, and always smiling. He seemed to not have any care in the world, and everything was available to him at his disposal. I too wanted that feeling. I wanted to feel on top of the world while being protected and loved. I wanted those things with Justin.

 We pulled up to a small house, looking as though it was being worked on but still in livable conditions. A two bedroom with a living room, bathroom and a kitchen, it was big enough and furnished to suite his needs, later learning it was the house he reserved for his business. "Is this your house?" I asked, trying to control the conversation before it instantly turned up to something hot and heated. I was still feeling nervous, trembling as the young girl in me began to come out. I may have been experienced, but never with anyone older than a teenager.

I followed behind as he led us through the front door and over to the sofa that was in front of a big, picture window. I was unable to sit still, fidgeting with everything within reach as I sat on the very end, allowing so much space between us you would have thought we were complete strangers. I never felt the feelings I was feeling, being in a room alone with the opposite sex whom I was beyond attracted to.

He grabbed a cheap bottle of whiskey and one plastic cup. "You want some of this?" he asked. I'm not old enough to drink, I thought in the back of my head, sitting in silence as my heart began to sink. He sat next to me, very close, and poured a little in the cup. Leaning forward, he placed it against my lips before slowly tilting it so the alcohol could flow into my mouth. Allowing him full control, I drank all of it, licking my lips of the drop left behind. He poured more and took a sip before reaching over me to place the cup on the end table. I was feeling good and relaxed; the alcohol settling in quickly on my adolescent body, creating a feeling beyond a level of comfort. Neither of us said a word and for the first time, I was experiencing the effects of alcohol. I looked over to notice Justin placing what appeared to be a pill into his mouth. "What is that?"

"Nothing." He took a swig from the bottle before reaching for my arm and pulling me close to him. He kissed me softly and gently, his left hand caressing my face as his right rubbed my thigh. Refusing to admit I was afraid, I placed both hands to my side as I leaned in to keep the kiss going. Still technically a virgin, I allowed for him to do whatever he wanted to me, with no cares in the world and wanting every minute to last. As time went on, I was ready to skip the life of being a teenager and dive straight into being an adult, until I found out I was pregnant on my sixteenth birthday.

Chapter 6

Just because we have been broken into little pieces does not mean we cannot be put back together. Our past does not define who we are nor does it determine where we are going. Although it took years for me to realize I was not in control, I knew there was a purpose for my existence. The devastations I faced were all for a reason and soon I would establish my identity.

Nay, in all these things we are more than conquerors through Him that loved us.

Romans 8:37 KJV

Despite our upbringing, our disfunctions, and our mistakes, we still have a purpose. My guidance was flawed, and I felt constant rejection. I experienced loss of close loved ones, left to grieve all alone. I craved attention and did not care what form it showed itself. A parent's absence and a lack of love will have you searching for all the wrong things in all the wrong places, picking up some bad habits along the way. I did not want to experience the financial hardship I watched my own mother go through, which led me to promiscuity, drug abuse, and eventually, self-destruction. My prayer life was nonexistent, lacking knowledge of how to overcome and live in true freedom. As I would always hear the older people say, "He may not come when you want Him, Be He's always on time", but if only I was curious enough back then to find out how mighty He truly was. I was still experiencing the current that would ultimately shift my life into a whole new direction in

His timing. He already knew the trials I would face on my journey in life. He was already prepared for the rejection I would constantly give Him before realizing it was Him carrying me through all the storms. Though I often felt judged and condemned, I continued to ignore the captivity and bondage on my life, giving into constant temptations of the flesh. I was weak and distracted.

The next morning, I was awakened by a knock at the front door. I looked up at the clock to notice it was only half past nine. Slowly I got up and located my robe, walking to the door as I noticed a floral van parked out front. When I opened the door, there was a man standing with a huge bouquet of sunflowers. "Are you Corrie Matthews?"

"Yes, I am Corrie, who are these from?" Not hesitating, I reached for the card. It read, *'just because I was thinking of you!'*. Although it was none other than a reminder of my poor judgements, I accepted the delivery, throwing the beautiful arrangement in the trash afterwards. Every year around Mother's Day I received a bouquet of flowers from Vanessa, my biological daughter, assuming they were really sent from her father. I left her over to Justin's house one night and never looked back, telling him I was going to the store for more pampers. At the age of seventeen, I could barely care for myself and my parents were already angry enough with having to deal with me. At first, I wanted to keep a relationship with her, not wanting her to feel abandoned as I did as a child. But as time passed, I could only selfishly focus on my wants and needs, and the thought of her became more of just a memory.

Grabbing only an apple from the refrigerator, I decided to throw on gym clothes to work off some stress before my first appointment at the spa, working out for what felt like hours. Whenever I felt uneased or bothered by something, the gym was the best stress reliever. I was spiritually empty and possessed no knowledge of the only way to true, divine peace.

After freshening up, I drove to the other side of town where my shop was located. I received a good tip from an old broker friend of mine, who was also a regular in the club, on this foreclosure in a nice, upscale area. Nick put up the funds as a business loan, but he never said anything about payments.

Jason, my first client of the day, was already sitting in the parking lot waiting on me when I arrived. Greeting him with a smile, I asked for fifteen minutes to set up. Although he was early, he looked aggravated for the wait. But it was no concern to me, considering he was one of my regulars and how easily clients were to come by. I unlocked the door and quickly set up my table, also lighting a few candles to set the mood. After dimming the lights, I opened the door to signal for him to come in.

A normal full body massage cost my clients anywhere between two to three hundred dollars per hour session. And to go all the way, as most of my clients always wanted to do, was five hundred. My prices were nonnegotiable and went up at my discretion. I operated out of a very secluded area and I was also a licensed massage therapist. The techniques I used were skilled. Not to mention, my clients had a lot of money. They were doctors, prosecutors, judges, and entrepreneurs who did not mind paying extra for pleasure and discretion. You would be surprised whom I entertained on a weekly basis. I had a website set up for my massage services and all others were by word of mouth.

Once I was done with Jason, I quickly cleaned up and showered to get ready for Michael. He did not like the idea of following behind another man, having to pretend he was my first client for the day. I normally tried to schedule that way, but Jason insisted on taking an early lunch.

I placed on my all leather, one-piece suite along with my stiletto heels. Michael was a dominatrix type of guy and liked it rough. Hearing a knock at the door, I grabbed my whip and walked seductively to answer it. "Who is it?" I spoke softly in my sexy, schoolgirl voice. Standing behind the door, I opened it slowly to allow for him to come in but before I could close it, another man followed. "I hope you don't mind. I brought one of my colleagues to meet you. He won't be staying long but I wanted him to meet you face to face."

A little annoyed by the unannounced visitor, I smile and reach out my hand to shake his. "Michael, you know I prefer to be told these things ahead of time and all appointments are made with Darla before being invited to my place of business." Still smiling, I remained professional, setting a mental reminder to get on to my receptionist about allowing unknowns in the back. In this profession, there were guidelines and rules to go by. If they could not maintain discretion, they were let go and no longer allowed back into my facilities.

"I do apologize", the other gentleman exclaimed.

"It is not your fault, but Michael knows the rules." I handed him my card while showing him to the door. "I work by appointments only. No phone calls allowed after 6 p.m. and if you leave a voice message it must contain only a name and phone number for call back, never any details." There was a business phone set up in the office for scheduling and a part time receptionist just to make things look more professional and legit. She maintained the front for the legal portion of the business and all my illegal clientele, as I would often refer to them, are directed to the back.

Once I was completely done at the office, I decided to go to the club to hang out. It was my off day, but I did not have much of anything to do at that point.

Once arriving, I walked straight to the bar and told Liz, the bartender, to give me a patron on the rocks. As usual, it was a full house, with no available tables in sight. Deslyn walked up behind me and sat on the barstool next to mine. She and I have known one another for a very long time. Taking me under her wing as a rookie, she inspired me to hustle much harder to become the head of my own empire. She was my biggest supporter as I became her number one protégé. Club owner by day, but a madam by night, she stood five feet eleven inches tall, light caramel complexion, curvy body, slender waist, green eyes, long, slender legs and D cup breast. Most people referred to her as Red Duchess, hence the club name 'The Duchess'. Half Puerto Rican, half black, no one suspected her as a solicitor of sex. "You don't want to work tonight? I have lots of guys asking for you." With a smirk on her face and look of ulterior motive, she stared in my eyes awaiting my response. Any other night I would agree but not that night. "I'll pass", I said with a smile on my face. "I would much rather be the audience for this one night." Sarcastically, she replied, "there is a two-drink minimum", as she got up from her seat then walked off. I knew she was joking but I already planned on having much more than two drinks. I waved Liz over to get me another and then another. Before realizing it, I was five drinks in and feeling very tipsy. I reached in my purse for a Xanax for an enhancement. Tasha, a new dancer, walked up right when I put it in my mouth and swallowed. She took a seat next to me and ordered a drink. "What's up girl? What are you doing in here on your off day?"

Tasha was a newbie. She had only been working at the club for a couple of weeks. However, the more I thought about it, I never seen her dancing. Maybe she was just a hostess or something. Just from looking at her I would not think she would defile herself in a way I was doing. Weighing no more than a buck twenty, she had long, straight black hair and hazel brown eyes. She was a very beautiful woman if I would say so myself.

"I just wanted to get out of the house. I didn't have much to do tonight", I replied. When in all actuality, I was taking a break from the full shift I just served at the spa and my grown lady parts could not take much more in one day.

"Yeah, I feel you. My shift has ended but my ride isn't here so I'll just chill with you." She ordered another drink as we continued to chat and laugh. The club closed at four, but we were still talking. Everyone already cleared out and Jeff, the bouncer, was walking our way.

"You ladies alright? It looks like you both need a cab!" We giggled and acted as though he was not standing beside us. I had such an enjoyable time just hanging out, I did not want to go home to an empty house. Never could I have imagined being a part of such a union. Although I decided not to entertain the idea of having friends, nobody enjoyed the feeling of being lonely. We all know rejection, pain, heartache, and loneliness. I thought by shutting everyone out, I could avoid all those things, but instead, I was blocking the people God was sending my way to help and lead me back to Him.

"No, no! We're both fine Jeff." I stood up and grabbed my purse. "It has definitely been fun guys. I will see you tomorrow." Tasha was still sitting there. Only now, she was constantly looking down at her watch. "Do you need a ride? It does not look like yours is coming". With gratitude, she immediately accepted my invitation without hesitating.

"I'll walk you fine ladies out", Jeff said as he placed his arms around our shoulders.

Once outside, we told him goodbye then got into my navy blue 2014 Dodge charger. The windows were as dark of a tint that the state would allow. "So where to?", I asked. Realizing I offered someone a ride with no idea where I was going. Tasha did not say a word. Instead, she began dialing a number on her phone while motioning for me to wait a second. "No answer", she said disappointingly. Her mood went from happy to upset and I knew I needed to intervene very quickly. "How about we get a bottle of wine and go to my house? You can crash with me for the night. It will be so much fun, like a slumber party." She nodded her head and we were on our way.

Tasha and I blasted the radio and partied the whole way there, not seeming like it was five thirty in the morning. We were both wired and ready to party the night away. I stopped at the corner store and minutes later we were pulling into my driveway.

"Girl, you must get really generous tips to have a spot like this!" I laughed it off, assuming if she really knew what I was in to she would probably judge me more harshly.

When we entered, Tasha sat on the sofa in the living room while I grabbed us some glasses. "So how long have you been at the club?" she asked, still curious to how I could afford something so fancy. My home was nearly three thousand square feet, custom built with four bedrooms and three baths. Brazilian, walnut flooring stretched from wall to wall with custom made furniture throughout. So busy building my lavish lifestyle, it was part of the reason why I chose to not have friends.

"I have been at the club since I was eighteen. Deslyn was kind of like my mentor who looked out for me."

"Eighteen?! You weren't old enough to work at the club. Where's your family?" She stared at me with an intriguing look in her eyes as I began to feel judged and condemned for my frowned upon ways. I could tell she wanted to hear my story. It was a story I could barely share with my therapist, yet, I could see the desire for some sort of connection in her eyes. Either that or I had too much to drink in one night. I decided to pour a glass of wine and entertain the possibilities.

"I am from Alabama but grew up in New York." She nodded her head but did not make a sound. Taking sips of wine from her glass, she waited patiently as I continued to speak. "I moved to Tampa at the age of eighteen with nothing and I have no family, so I did what I had to do to survive." I took the last swallow of my wine and poured another glass. I didn't know her well enough to give a full disclosure, deciding to shift the conversation off myself.

"So, what about you? What's your story?"

A little hesitant, Tasha replies, "I'm just a nobody trying to make it."

I thought to myself, aren't we all!

Chapter 7

For this is the will of God, even your sanctification, that ye should abstain from fornication.

1Thessalonians 4:3 KJV

I slept into the late afternoon with no interruptions. Tasha eventually found someone to come pick her up, but admittingly, I enjoyed having someone to talk to. I did not want to volunteer too much information since it was my first night really getting to know her, but I felt like we could possibly develop some sort of friendship.

I dragged for what little time I did have to myself before going into my appointments. Going to bed so late and having so much to drink did not agree with me. I felt like my body did not get enough rest and I was sluggish. I started a pot of coffee and sat on the sofa to check the messages in my inbox. I must have been sleeping very hard because I had three missed calls, all from Nick. The first two messages were very nonchalant but in the third one I could tell he was becoming aggravated. I was curious to know what he wanted but, needing more time to work on my schedule, I was not too eager to call right back. Instead, I rushed to the shower.

My first appointment of the day was Jessie. Although far from an athlete, his physique was muscular. He had always been a very good lay and one of my clients whom I enjoyed pleasuring. The size of his package gave me instant bursts of orgasms and I knew he enjoyed giving it to me as much as I enjoyed my job of receiving him. I imagined him being mine and every time my job was complete, I would lean over to kiss his lips, remembering to seem engaged minus the emotions. But once we were done, he had a wife to go home to. Every time we had sex, he never took his ring off and would politely excuse himself whenever she was to call. Those were the moments that reminded me of my role as a high-priced prostitute, and never the main chick. Once done, Jessie paid me and left in a hurry to get home while I hung around to wash up. I had five more clients scheduled back to back, some were for full service with others only wanting oral, and then I would be off to the club.

I arrived at Duchess around a quarter to eleven. After drinking an entire pot of coffee, I was wide awake and ready to make more money. My hustle was strong, and I could not get enough. I wanted it all. As I walked through the club I smiled and said hello to everyone, making sure to not leave anyone feeling left out. I immediately changed clothes and hit the floor, working harder than I would any other night. I knew I wanted more for my life, but the fast money just kept pulling me back in. It was something I knew I could be great at without having to try so hard.

At the end of my shift the only thing I wanted to do was crawl into bed. Everyone had cleared the club and I was minutes away from leaving the dressing room when Tasha walked in. She seemed to always just show up out of nowhere. Standing there half naked with dollars hanging out of my thong, all I could think about was putting on my clothes so she could no longer stare at my erect nipples. I decided to make small talk to take all the attention from my actions.

"What are you doing here? I haven't seen you all night." I walked over to my locker and grabbed my clothes, hurriedly to place them on my body.

"You're not embarrassed, are you?" Tasha asked jokingly. And although I was, I quickly replied, "Girl no! I just wasn't expecting anyone to walk in here." I seldom pleasured women at my shop but I was still ignorant to whether a woman was hitting on me or not.

She walked over to the mirror to check her makeup while I was dressing. Uncertain to why she was there, I decided to ask again. "So, what brings you this way at closing hours?"

"You!" She looked at me with a concerned smirk on her face.

Now I was confused. Her intentions were not clear, so I gave her a puzzled look. "I was thinking you and I could go get some drinks or hang out at your house like last night."

"That's cool. Just let me finish wrapping up in here and you can follow me. I have some tequila in my cabinet I haven't even touched yet." She smiled. "Cool! I'll meet you outside.

When Tasha and I arrived at my house, Nick was at my doorstep with flowers. I felt bad for having her drive all this way just to turn around, but something was wrong if he was popping up at my house unannounced. And what was even more puzzling, there was no car parked in the yard. I intercepted Tasha before she could step a foot out of her car. "I'm so sorry but I'm going to have to take a rain check. I really wasn't expecting to have company tonight." Tasha gave me a look of understanding and placed her car in reverse. I then turned towards the front door with excitement. The fact of me having a long day and wanting to go to bed no longer mattered. Regardless of the situation, the outcome was going to be a very happy ending with the man whom I truly loved.

"I thought you were never going to come home. I've been waiting for an hour now. And I know you have been getting the missed phone calls." He was standing there in some rugged, denim jeans and a white t-shirt. Sweat was running down his face and you could see the wetness seeping through his shirt. I was feeling more seductive than I had been all day because the one man I wanted to seduce was standing right in front of me. I gave him a warm inviting hug and kiss. "What was that for?"

"You should come in and find out." I smiled, biting my bottom lip. As we walked inside, I could feel his eyes all over me.

"Who was the woman following you home?"

I turned around to notice his eyes all over me. "That was a new girl from the club. She wanted to hang out and chat."

He gave me a puzzling look. "I already don't care for your choice of profession and I don't see you on a regular, but all I'm telling you is to be careful. I love you and I don't trust those girls at that club. It's not like you to…." I cut him off.

"Repeat what you just said."

With hesitation he replies, "What I say? Which part?"

"The part about you loving me". I was smiling so hard my cheeks felt like they were on fire. It meant so much to me to hear those words come out of his mouth. He had always been my biggest supporter since day one. Never did he pass judgement or degrade me for what I chose to do. He stood by my side and had my back the entire time. Rather than dwelling on the time we didn't have, I decided to enjoy the moments we did and when Nick and I had awakened, it was one in the afternoon. We both laid there holding one another, the room still pitch black from the dark curtains I kept over my windows. Believing Nick wanted to be here with me, never did I expect an ulterior motive.

"Corrie, I need you to loan me twenty." While I knew he wasn't talking about twenty dollars, all I could wonder was, what kind of mess had he gotten into now. I laid silently and motionless. As much as I loved Nick, I loved my money much more. And even though he could have easily said, I owed it to him, it was still my money. But I did not desire to know the situation and refused to be a witness to his illegal activities. Whether he owed someone or was making a flip, neither was my business. I decided to give it to him, knowing he would have done the same for me.

To avoid reporting to the bank, he already knew he would not receive all twenty thousand in a lump sum. We had to break it down into smaller increments over a certain period. I slid out of his arms and walked over to my closet, making a withdrawal from the safe. Pulling out a five-thousand-dollar stack of one hundred-dollar bills, I tossed it over to him while he was still laying comfortably under the covers.

"I'll have to get the rest for you later. You know how it works."

And afterwards, I crawled back into bed, in his arms. I wanted him back in my life, to be my man and to hold me like this every night but first needing to figure out a plan to end his marriage and draw him closer to me.

Chapter 8

"Therefore whosoever heareth these sayings of mine, and doeth them, I will liken him unto a wise man, which built his house upon a rock: And the rain descended, and the floods came, and the winds blew, and beat upon that house; and it fell not: for it was founded upon a rock. And every one that heareth these saying of mine, and doeth them not, shall be likened unto a foolish man, which built his house upon the sand: And the rain descended, and the floods came, and the winds blew, and beat upon that house; and it fell: and great was the fall of it."

Matthew 7:24-27 KJV

The night was calm, and the stars shined so brightly in the sky. I could see the big, shiny moon and there was no cloud in sight. As I sat on my patio, sipping on a glass of Moscato wine, I thought about my past and what could have been. I considered my future and all the possibilities. But most importantly, I paid close attention to the right now. The previous night with Nick was magical and I wanted nothing more but to be able to live that life forever. For so many years I played the role of the victim, wanting to blame any and every one for my problems and mistakes. I wallowed in misery over a loss that happened years ago instead of building on the relationships I had at that very moment. And my outlet, letting men take advantage of my body day in and day out.

No, I had never perceived myself as perfect; I did not intend to be. But for that one night, I could really dig deep down and ask myself, who was Corrie? Had I become just another statistic in society whom people looked at indifferently because of my lifestyle? I had put so much time and effort into building an empire of financial stability. Never wanting to give up what I started, I neglected to realize, what goes up will one day come crashing down if it is not built on a stable foundation. The only thing I had was sex, money, and lies. The body I flaunt around, I would not have forever, and I did not think Des was investing in my retirement plan. Furthermore, I never even considered a life insurance policy.

That morning as I was flipping through the paper, I read a story about the police finding body parts of a dismembered stripper. The remains were found in several garbage bags after concerned residents reported a foul odor coming from the house next door. She was missing for two days and her parents were clueless of the lifestyle she was living. It made me think about all the innocent faces at amateur night, impatiently waiting on their three minutes of fame. Yet, they had no idea of the life they were so eager to jump headfirst into. The story brought tears to my eyes but made me think. I remained naïve in my own life, never taking into consideration the danger it may or may not cause. The sad story of it all was the fact, I was once those young girls. Making thousands of dollars in one week brought excitement to my life as well. When you come from nothing and you are raised as nothing, it is easy to think of your life as meaningless. It is easy to be sucked into the wickedness of the world, believing easy money is the best outlet.

I finished off my glass of wine before calling it a night. My heart was heavy, and my mind grew deeper into thought by the minute. I laid in the dark, contemplating. What if that were me? What if I had been the girl whom body parts they found in those bags? No one would even care that I was gone. All the long, exhausting nights of shaking my butt in the clubs and having sex for money would not have meant anything.

In that industry, I was far from irreplaceable. I came a dime a dozen and it was proven to me every Wednesday when girls much younger than I came flaunting their half-naked bodies into the club ready to take it all off for a chance to win five hundred dollars and a job. But were they really winning? Or were they just being sucked into Deslyn's trap to build her empire and put more money in her pockets? These questions weighed heavily on my mind and I realized at some point in my life my body was going to be worn. I would no longer be as appealing. One day I would not be the most talked about dancer in the club. And at some point, those attorneys, judges, businessmen, and entrepreneurs were going to want something new. But at that moment, the show had to continue.

My cell phone rang at a quarter to three in the morning. Although I should have been asleep, my wondering mind would not allow it. I picked up the phone to notice an unknow, New Orleans phone number. Assuming it was Nick, I answered.

"I know he was there with you." A woman's voice had rung out from the other end. She was crying and screaming at the same time, immediately realizing it was Leslie, Nick's wife. Although I had no interest in entertaining this conversation, I held the phone and listened as she expressed how she was feeling.

"Why won't you just go away? Just leave my family alone. He is my husband you piece of trash!"

Feeling no remorse, I did not understand why she would choose now, of all times, to call me. For years she would make small comments about me being a homewrecker and how I needed to find my own man, but never has she called me directly. I could only assume the feelings she kept bottled up inside finally gotten the best of her. And suddenly, in the wee hours of the early morning, she was calling my phone. I knew what Nick and I had done was wrong. But it takes two. Never did he express to me a lack of interest, nor did I force him into my bed. The empathy she was seeking was not there and the issue she had was not with me, it was with Nick.

Nonchalantly I replied, "why don't you go enjoy your husband? I sure did." And before I knew it, I hung up in her face, immediately placing her on the block list. I felt vindicated and justified, unbothered by the idea of ruining a marriage, a holy matrimony made between two people and God. Instead, I was intrigued by the fact she would take the time out of her schedule to call my phone with the issues between her and Nick. In my mind, I was not the problem. My feelings would not allow for me to feel nor understand what she was feeling because it was not me on the other end. I had no idea what it felt like to be cheated on because I was the other woman. After losing both, my brother and my mother, I became numb to the idea of feeling anything close to sympathetic for another person. Pain, anger, and frustration were feelings of my past which I vowed to never experience again. I learned to put up a block and keep it moving for the sake of my livelihood. There was no time for those temporary feelings when there was money to be made, and lots of it.

Feeling unbothered, I rolled over with a smirk on my face, imagining how the rest of the morning would go for her and Nick. Thirty minutes later, my phone began to ring again. Out of aggravation, I answered this time without even looking at the caller id. It was Leslie again. Not even giving me time to say hello, she began to talk as soon as I pressed the button to answer. She was not crying nor screaming anymore. Instead, she was calm.

"Karma is a mother and you reap what you sew."

Not saying another word, she hung up. And I continued to lay there, holding the phone to my ear as though I was waiting for someone to continue to speak. I realized she had called me from Nick's cell and my heart dropped. Could he have known she was calling me or was he still asleep as she secretly called me from his phone? Assuming the worse, I made a mental note to call him as soon as the sun came up to find out what was really going on. Never did I ask him to fly down here and I know he could not have just played me for sex one last time just to cut me loose afterwards. After minutes of deep thought, my body finally decided to call it a night as I dozed off.

Chapter 9

The next morning, I felt rejuvenated and, although I planned on giving Nick a ring, I left it alone. I was not about to let the shenanigans of their broken marriage ruin my hustle. There were more important things to think about. Putting on a pot of coffee, I turned the radio on and began my morning routine. Grabbing my cell phone, I first checked my bank accounts, followed by my social media accounts, and then I proceeded to get dressed so that I could entertain some clients before going to the club.

Life for me seemed simple. I had no friends, no family, nor any significant others, which made it much easier to become engaged in things of me and whatever I desired to do with my time. My spa gave me the opportunity to bond with the opposite sex, fulfilling their fantasies while creating my own. But when I was at the club, I pretended it was just a typical night on the town, clubbing, dancing, and having the time of my life before going home and crashing alone. Never giving any thought to how routine my life truly was, I avoided being caught up in my emotions.

Finishing up my last client, I cleaned up and decide to go to the gym before my shift at the club. Once I arrived, I walk in to find Tasha running on the treadmill. Ironically enough, I was starting to feel like I was being stalked. Ever since the night at the club, I could not seem to get rid of her. It was as if she was seeking a friendship, and I was her target.

Before I could maneuver my way back out of the door, she threw her hand up, signaling for me to come over, never slowing down the pace of her run. With a smile and attempting not to let her see how annoyed I was, I walk over to say hello.

"Hey girl, I didn't know you were a member at this gym." Nor did I think you would be over in this area; I was thinking to myself.

Never being the type to make small talk, I was looking for a way out. She had been too generous for me to be rude and I could not make an excuse to leave because I just walked through the door, no sweat in sight. Instead, I climbed on the machine next to her and began to jog at a slow pace. My communication skills were rusty and starting a conversation was not my specialty but if you put me in a room with a bunch of horny, egotistical men, I could surely become the life of the party.

"What have you been up to?" She was running while attempting to hold a conversation, but my lungs would not allow for me to do both at the same time. I had to choose between running or talking and judging from the lack of topics there were to discuss between the two of us, I chose to continue running. "Nothing" was all I could say while keeping up with her pace. I usually preferred the weights just because that was where all the sexy guys worked out.

Thirty minutes in, I needed a break. I pressed the cool down button on my machine as Tasha continued to run as if she was preparing for a marathon. There was something about her that I could not put my finger on, but she was not your ordinary woman, and for the life of me, I could not understand what it was she did in the club. I never saw her dancing, she didn't really fraternize with the men, nor did she carry herself as someone who took her clothes off for them. It seemed as if she was more interested in my life, when coming over the other night, and she never opened about hers. Now here she was popping up everywhere I went with no explanation to the why's. I was beyond confused but I did not know the right questions to ask to get the information I needed out of her. But she was very good at prying information out of me. Who was she really? Any why was she continuously digging for information?

When she noticed I was about to stop, she hurriedly stopped her machine and began to follow me to the showers. After thirty minutes of running, I concluded that to be the end of my work out for the day. I was not interested in anything else. Matter of fact, I was contemplating calling out from the club. All I wanted to do was go home and crawl into my bed.

"Where are you going after this? Want to grab a bite?"

In my mind, I was rolling my eyes to the idea of sitting through a meal with her just because I knew she would ask a lot of questions. However, I did not want to be rude and obnoxious. Considering I no longer desired to work tonight, it did not hurt to get something to eat with Tasha before calling it a night. After all, a girl still needed to have dinner.

"Let me call Des to let her know I won't be working tonight and then we can go grab a bite."

Tasha hopped in the shower as I sat on the bench, digging in my bag to get my cell phone. To my surprise, there were eight missed calls, all from the club. There were no voicemails nor any text, but I knew something was wrong. Whenever Des had a problem she would call me. I grabbed my bag and hurried to my car to go find out what was going on. Never did I think to tell Tasha, my mind was on the club and how my money could possibly be affected. I was certain she would understand the hustle.

When I arrived, I parked in my usual parking spot and proceeded towards the entrance. From the looks of it, the club was near empty. I spotted Des and Jeff having a, what seem like serious, conversation. In the past thirteen years, never had I seen the look I was seeing on that day. I was afraid to speak to either of them and they were too engaged to notice my arrival. I approached the bar where Liz was standing to find out what I missed.

"Girl, what's going on?"

Without hesitation she replied, "Deslyn is being audited for tax fraud. The club is closed until further notice."

"What!" I was in shock. That explained why the club was so empty and Des was so upset. Just like myself, anything that made her lose money was enough to send her over the edge. I began to ask as many questions as Liz would allow for me to ask.

"All I know is, three guys entered the club in fancy suites waiving around badges. Minutes later everyone was cleared out and Des was scrambling around trying to hide documents."

Even though it was an unfortunate situation, all I could think about was how I was being affected. I did not want to imagine the hundreds I was going to lose a night until Des could get the club back open, if she would be able to reopen. My selfishness kicked in and I was becoming angry, one of the emotions I avoided for so long. I made it my business to turn the situation around and make it selfishly enough about me. Not caring about how any of the others would be affected nor about how some of these girls would be able to keep their lights on without this job, I immediately began to think about all the money I just gave to Nick and I wanted it back.

Tasha came rushing into the club a little shortly after me. She looked concerned and was trying to console Des. I did not avoid eye contact, but I knew she was wondering why I did not give her the heads up before leaving the gym. I guess she must have received the news from someone else. But instead of being angry, she was still her happy-go-lucky self who she had always been since the day I first met her. She never missed a beat. Walking over to where Liz and I were, she expressed her desire to want to help.

"Are you ladies going to be ok? Do you have other resources to help provide until all of this mess is cleaned up?"

Instead of going into details, I just smiled and nodded my head. Some things are better kept unsaid and the last thing I needed was for Tasha to pop up at my spa just to find me giving some random sexual favors to a client.

Changing the subject, I suggested we take a ride over to Clearwater so we all could clear our minds. Although Liz declined, wanting to hang around in case her services were needed to put up the last of the alcohol, I knew Tasha would be all in. But first we stopped by my house, so she could park her car. Neither of us felt comfortable with her leaving it at the club, mostly my reasons were because I was not interested in having to drive her back. Once we arrived at my house, she parked her car and jumped into the passenger seat of mine.

"Co, I have no idea what I am supposed to do for money now that the club is closed." Knowing Des will be eager to get the money to reopen the club, I was certain she would come for me to help. I guess when money calls some of us answer, and swiftly. I began to wonder, how, after these years, did the IRS find out about her schemes. Not knowing how close Des and I truly were, Tasha has been the only other dancer I allowed in my circle. Mostly because she insisted on being a part of my life. Unlike the others, I carried myself as a businesswoman, not as a stripper. Unless I disclosed to someone, I took my clothes off for a living, they would never have been able to guess. Those are pointers Des taught me early in the game and the reason why I was able to outlast the rookies who were in and out within five years.

When we arrived at the restaurant, I spotted Nick sitting in the corner with another woman. They were laughing and giggling very loudly while his hand was on her knee. My heart broke, and my eyes became very watery. My immediate assumption was that I had been played and taken advantage of. Although I was very aware of Nick's slick ways, never in a million years would I have expected for him to turn it around and use it against me.

"Something wrong Corrie? You look like you just lost your puppy." Tasha began to show deep concern as she placed her hand on my shoulder.

I was speechless. I could not move nor, would any words come out of my mouth. I was so hurt I could not decide if I wanted to sit or leave. Trying to understand why life was not getting any better, I walked over to the table to make my presence known.

Tasha walked up behind me looking confused. Before I could say anything, she opened her mouth to say it for me. "Isn't this the guy who was at your doorstep at two in the morning the other night?" I looked at Nick as the tears began to stream down my cheeks. I no longer desired to eat at that restaurant nor did I want to continue standing there feeling foolish. And Tasha completely understood because she was walking out right behind me.

The entire ride home was completely silent. I did not want to talk about it, nor did I desire to listen to the coincidental love songs that were on every station. I knew Nick could never be mine, he was married. My heart felt so much pain and I kept asking myself if I had set myself up for this one. I knew Nick and I were not officially together but the mixed signals and the night we shared reassured me that the love was still there. Or at least that is what I wanted to believe. I felt played. I cleared out my savings for him and now with the club closing, I had no resources to fall back on.

"Co, I'm not leaving you alone. I know you don't want to talk, and I completely understand. But it is not healthy for you to be here all by yourself after the day you just experienced."

It was nice of Tasha to hang around to make sure everything was going to be ok. Once entering the house, she grabbed her cell phone to order take out. "They'll be here in thirty to forty minutes. Do you still have that tequila from the other night?"

I began to sob even harder at just the thought of the other night. That was the night Nick and I made passionate love for hours. I was afraid things would result to what transpired, never asking Nick to clarify where I stood with him. Because of our history, I felt automatically entitled to his heart and most importantly, his loyalty. Mainly it was because I did not want to choose between my career and my love life. Ever since we started hanging out again, he had not said anything about the club. I felt like it was partly my fault because I was having sex with a married man, expecting him to leave her and committing to me. But I could never admit to it, too naïve to realize he was still standing his ground on how he felt. Basically, I was just sex to him unless I called for something, or in his case, if he called to borrow money. Although wanting to believe he still felt something in his heart for me, it was time to move on, for good.

Chapter 10

For hours, my phone rang nonstop. It went from Nick to Leslie all day, Nick trying to plead his case and Leslie cursing out my voicemail. They both kept leaving message after message, but I had no interest in what neither wanted to tell me. Tasha was staying at my house to keep me company. Des called to inform me of the ongoing investigation, but I did not let Tasha know of our communication.

After three days of sitting in the house, cleaning, thinking, and then more cleaning, I decided to get dressed and attend a therapy session. I called to beg for a last-minute appointment. As depressing as reality had become, I could not lose focus. I dressed in my turquoise and white maxi dress with some white sandals, grabbed my purse and drove to the doctor's office.

For the first time, I did the speed limit so I could think. I wanted to feel free and forget about all that happened days ago, becoming very aware of the circumstances between Nick and myself. I realized having sex only made it worse. Since the club was closed, all I had was my spa. But in the end, there was a possibility I could lose everything.

I pulled up to the office, let out a deep sigh, and then proceeded to the entrance. The receptionist at the counter politely greeted me while handing me a clipboard. "Ms. Matthews, if you could just please fill out these papers. We've made some changes recently and need to have this in our file. You can just hand it to Dr. Hunt when she calls you back." I glanced over the paper as I sat in the closest seat I could find. It looked completely like the forms I filled out three months ago. What changes could they have possibly made? I reached for a pen in my purse and began to fill out as much as possible. Once completed, I went back to the first page where it read, please check all the following symptoms or thoughts that apply to you now or during the past six months. I must have marked more than half of the options, not able to remember what I marked on the questionnaire three months ago. As soon as I finished, Dr. Hunt called me back.

"Good afternoon Corrie. It has been a long time. How are you today?"

I handed her the clipboard while replying. "Life is life." I was really trying not to think about everything. I lost my job and the love of my life all in one day. Everyone goes through trials and tribulations, but I felt I had come to a crossroad in my life and could not bear anymore heartache. I sat down on the sofa without waiting on Dr. Hunt to tell me where to sit. "So how are you doing?" I asked. I could tell I caught her off guard and she was not expecting me to ask. "Well Ms. Matthews, not one person is perfect, but the day is only as great as you make it." Although she always had quotes of positivity, today seemed a little different. She was displaying a blank look on her face as though her world was crumbling in as she pondered on life, never seeing her look depressed. But then again, I had not been coming like I should. Many assume that therapist and counselors do not have problems, otherwise, how could they possibly fix someone else? For a very long time I was that person. I had been told constantly to seek help and, in my defense, I would argue that those type of people could not do much to help me. They were human with problems as well.

I wanted to break something. I wanted to yell and scream to the top of my lungs until the pain went away, but what purpose did that serve? Life was no different than it was back then. The only difference was the amount of money in my bank account and the size of my house with no one to share it all with. It did not buy me happiness, nor did it make me feel any differently about the people in my life.

Walking out of my therapy session, I rushed to my car for my stress reliever, Xanax. Since the day I found out about Jamal's death, nothing had been able to bring me relief besides those pills. My life felt empty without them. One of my clients was a doctor and gave me unlimited prescriptions in exchange for a discount off his bills. I thought about asking Dr. Hunt for them, just in case he and I had fallen out and my supply was depleted but most likely she would have denied me. I would have to show some signs of anxiety or have panic attacks for her to even have considered it.

Chapter 11

At what point do you realize your worth, your true value to life?

How many times does it take to right your wrongs without making the same mistake twice?

Why are we expected to remain strong through all the burdens and grief?

When the pressure continues to build, and you cannot find relief.

The heart becomes cold with no more love to give,

Looking in the mirror,

I know it is myself whom I need to forgive.

I'm too sensitive, too possessive, wanting to control everything around me,

*Self-consciously knowing perfect is
something I never will be.*

*Ashamed of the person whom I have become,
I shriek in disgust.*

*How can one give love when self I cannot
trust?*

The next few weeks were a blur. Thinking the club would reopen in only a matter of days, there was no word on the status. I felt betrayed by Nick and it became more and more obvious he set me up to get what he needed, or at least that is what my emotions were telling me. I could not think straight nor could I function. I needed to get away and the only place I could think of going was……. New York.

For some reason, I did not feel the need to inform anyone of my sporadic decision. After all, who would I have told? I spent the entire day packing. Not knowing how long I would stay, I packed half of my closet.

The next morning, I was up at the crack of dawn, organizing things around the house and double checking my luggage, making sure nothing important was forgotten before my flight. I put on a pot of coffee and bounced around to my Beyoncé CD. I began to play in my mind how I would react if I was to run into Justin, but my main thought was how my dad would react once he saw me. Never returning after high school, I had not spoken to him in years. The last I heard he was not doing too well. My stepmom reached out to me on social media a few months back, but I neglected to reply.

Interrupting my thoughts, the phone began to ring. I glanced at the caller ID but did not recognize the number. Ignoring all the possibilities, I continued to get dressed and load my luggage into the trunk of my car. Doubling back through the house, I wanted to make sure everything was turned off, secured, and locked. I reached for my keys and walked towards the front door. But once I opened it, I froze solid in my steps. Nick was standing there with a look of sadness on his face, right hand in midair, displaying a sign of "power to the people", but it was obvious he was getting ready to knock on the door as I intercepted.

"Co, we really need to talk, and I knew you would not answer any of my phone calls. Please just listen to me and if you never want to speak to me again afterwards, I completely understand but I must clear the air."

Clear the air? What was he talking about? He was having dinner with another woman who was not his wife after he just hustled me out of several thousands of dollars. Who was she, was the question lingering through my mind? I took a glance at my watch. It was ten thirty and I really needed to get to the airport.

"Nick, I really don't have time for this. I have a flight to catch and you have received all that you are going to get out of me. So, you and I have nothing more to say."

"We are back in Tampa for good." Nick yelled as I walked to the car. Unsure what response he would get out of me, I turned towards him in disbelief. I wanted to fight back tears but the thought of knowing I could see him anytime I wanted made me weak to my knees. Although I did not want to love him, it was impossible not to. I clearly had been overthinking things. Leslie knew how he felt about me, and I could only assume this move could not have been any parts of her idea.

"Unless you are going to be completely honest with me, you and I have nothing to talk about. You came to my home asking for money and then I see you in Clearwater with another woman, smiling in one another's face as if everything was ok. What am I supposed to expect Nick? How am I supposed to feel? You hurt me!"

The tears would not stop, and I did not want them to. Aside from the nonchalant, hustle mentality, I still had feelings. I was human just like anyone else. The only difference, I knew how to bottle it all in. I chose not to love, not to show empathy in any sort of way, and to put up a block around my emotions to prevent these types of things from happening. But no matter how much I tried to run; Nick always had a way of tearing down that wall. Now there we were, standing in my front yard, neither of us with a clue what would happen next. This was not a movie, only my real life being played out like some unrealistic love scene. He gazed at me with his handsome brown eyes, already knowing the question I wanted him to answer.

"She was my realtor. But why does it even matter to you? For years you have sent mixed signals. Even if I wasn't married, we both know you are incapable of commitment. You even left your own child in a different state with your baby daddy. You didn't want your own daughter!"

'You did not want your own daughter'……. I think those were the only words I heard coming from his mouth. And as upset as I was for him saying it, it was true. I gave up my child to continue to live my own life. And not because I was looking out for her best interest, but because I was selfishly focusing on mine. What did that really say about my character? And now Nick was standing there calling me out. It was not very often you would hear about the dead-beat mom who left her child. No…. it was more so the father who leaves the mother and child. But there I was, changing the dynamics of things and I could not even open my mouth to rebuttal. I was the dead-beat mother. I was the sorry mother who pushed my child away, so I could continue a lifestyle of selling my body for money, not worthy of being called 'mom'. Yet, I was pissed off at everyone else. I could not take much more of the conversation. Leaving Nick standing in the yard, I got into my car and backed out of the driveway without saying goodbye.

Chapter 12

I arrived at Rochester, New York's airport at a quarter to seven. The only thing on my mind was to get to the hotel and take a warm bath. After the morning I encountered, I could not bear to deal with anymore drama in one day. I spent approximately an hour at the rental car counter trying to obtain a vehicle. Although I made reservations, they were acting as though they did not have any availability. Rather than putting up a fuss, I settled for the next thing available because I could not wait any longer. The customer service representative handed me the keys to a Dodge Caliber as she continuously apologized for the inconvenience.

As soon as we got done with the inspection and I was settled, I set the GPS to the Hilton, adamant about being too far from the airport in case I decided not to keep the rental for the entire trip. Although I said I would visit my dad, that was not a definite.

When I arrived at the hotel, I could not help but notice the handsome gentleman sitting in the lobby. After making eye contact, I immediately turned my attention to the receptionist. "Good evening. I have a reservation for Corrie Matthews". I smiled and glanced back to see if the sexy, chocolate gentleman was still looking. I was glowing, starting to tingle all over. Mesmerized by his charming physique, I did not notice the lady attempting to hand me my door key. "He came in with a group of partners last night. I think they are here on a business meeting." She smiled as she gave me a wink. There was no hiding it, so obvious that everyone in the lobby had to have been feeling my vibes. I reached for the key and my luggage to walk towards the elevator but stopped in my steps by him.

"I'm Marcel. Can I help you with some of your belongings?" His voice was very deep and masculine. Standing there in disbelief, I could not move nor speak. I just smiled as he took that as a yes. Not wanting to come off as boogie, I was speechless. "Are you going to tell me your name, or do you not have one?" We both began to laugh. How silly of me to not say anything. I was so lost in his smile, his smell, and his gorgeous eyes.

"Hi, I'm Corrie." I reached out to shake his hand, not wanting to let go. His handshake was firm, yet, gentle to a woman's touch. I could tell he was attempting not to squeeze too tightly. This man was everything I looked for in a one-night stand and I yearned for him to pull me closer. It was obvious we shared a sexual attraction like none other and my body language was telling a story. He grabbed my luggage and I followed as he walked towards the elevators. Small talk was not really my niche, so I waited to see if he would start the conversation once we entered and the doors shut.

"So, what brings you to New York?" He displayed curiosity all over his face. Not wanting to disclose too much information, I knew I needed to be as discreet as I possibly could be. After all, this would be nothing more than a fun time. I would fly back to Tampa and he would return to wherever it was he came from with no need in trying to make the situation more than what it really was. So why was I overthinking things already?

"I'm here for a family reunion." I quickly thought of a lie to avoid the awkward pause between each of his questions. Although there was no family, nor a reunion. "What about yourself? Why are you here?"

"I am here for a couple of days with some partners from my law firm. We are wrapping up a case for a client."

I thought to myself, an attorney. I have had my share of sleeping with those type of guys but never one who showed real interest in me outside of sex. The rest of the conversation was more of him asking questions as I giggled like a high school girl being hit on by the star quarter back. I was so into him and it was all over my face, smiling from ear to ear all the way to my door.

"This is my room. Thanks for your assistance. I think I can take it from here."

"So, Corrie, do you have any big plans for tonight?"

"No, not at all." I replied quickly in hopes of him inviting me to his room for a little one on one.

"Well, I am in town for four days. Maybe we can get together for drinks or something."

"Sure!" I responded with no hesitation. "Just let me get settled and take a breather. I can meet you downstairs in about an hour."

He agreed and nodded with a smile. We said our goodbyes and I stood at my door, watching as he walked down the hall towards the elevator. I was so excited and full of energy.

Instead of unpacking, I left all my bags in the middle of the floor and decided to indulge in a hot bubble bath, needing to relax.

Once arriving downstairs, I immediately spotted Marcel sitting at the bar. He was dressed casually with some khaki slacks and a navy-blue polo style shirt. I stood, undressing him with my eyes for what seemed like a good five minutes before he got up to come escort me over to where he was sitting. I was wearing my pink maxi dress and black open toe flip flops. I did not feel the need to get fancy when I knew it would only be a matter of hours before it would all be coming off. There were no subliminal messages being displayed. Everything about me was saying, come and get it! Swaying my hips from side to side, I swayed my way over to the bar. "I'll have a caramel apple martini please." I told the bartender while observing the crowd around us before taking my seat. Marcel still had not taken his eyes off me, dissecting every inch of my curves. It was very flattering.

We made small talk, avoiding any conversation pertaining to my personal life. He did not need to know I was visiting in attempt to deal with my issues. My dysfunctional life was never anything to brag about. I just wanted to enjoy hanging out and having some drinks in hopes of it leading back to his hotel room.

Every time we would make eye contact, he just smiled. It was as though he already knew my intentions. In my opinion, there was nothing wrong with a one-night stand. After all, we were both adults. I glanced him up and down like he was some type of dessert I was dying to dive in to. "You see something you like?" He smiled with a teasing look on his face. He knew I wanted him more than anything at that moment. Waiving over the bartender, he requested another drink for the both of us. Although I was already feeling good and relaxed, another did not hurt. I placed my hand on his knee and worked it up towards his crotch, no need for any more stalling.

We both rushed the last drink. Marcel dropped a hundred-dollar bill on the bar as he grabbed me by the hand to lead me to the elevator, disregarding any change that was left. I became even more excited at what was about to happen. Not only did I want what he was serving, I felt I needed it more than anything. No thoughts of Tampa or what transpired earlier that day nor of any worries of what may happen once I come face to face with my dad. The only thing on my mind was that handsome man making me feel like a million bucks, even if it was only a temporary fix, wanting it to last all night and possibly into the early morning.

We staggered on to the elevator. I was feeling so tipsy and ready for whatever was to come. Marcel asked, "Your room or mine?" With the way I was feeling, we could have started in my room and ended in his. But I did not desire to put that idea on the table. I wanted him to take the lead. He reaches to press the number eight for the eighth floor. His room it was. Being the only two on the elevator, I was tempted to take him right there and he could not keep his hands off me, rubbing me all over.

Making our way down the hall to his room, I did not think twice about what was about to happen. He placed the card key into the door and opened it. My eyes widened as I stood there astonished. He was staying in an executive suite and everything he needed was right at his fingertips.

"What type of wine would you like?"

I turned towards him to realize he was on the phone. Too busy checking out his space, I did not notice he was calling room service.

"I prefer Moscato."

He placed the order, ordering wine and something else but I was so into my surroundings, I did not pay him any attention. Kicking off my shoes, I took my place on the huge king size bed. Not saying a word, he grabbed my feet and began to rub them. This man was doing everything right and he barely knew me. I was blown away by how delicate he was.

He mostly did all the talking but out of curiosity I finally decided to ask, "Where are you from?"

"I live in Atlanta, but I grew up in Savannah. Have you ever been to Georgia?"

He smiled about everything and never hesitated to answer any of my questions as he continued to massage my feet. "I've visited Atlanta once but never Savannah." I knew with me asking I needed to be willing to answer the same question, so I volunteered the information without giving him the opportunity. "I live in Tampa."

He looked surprised. "Really? I love Florida. With my busy schedule, I don't get to go as often as I would like but I hear

Tampa is beautiful. Maybe you could show me around whenever I get a chance to come down."

I laughed. As much as I would like to entertain the idea, I had enough men in my life to complicate things. Nick just moved back, and the club was at risk of closing for good. Still contemplating my plans for my life, I knew a relationship was not a part of those intentions. But there was nothing wrong with indulging in life for a moment.

"So, what do you do for a living? It must be something fulfilling if you can just take off and visit New York in the middle of the week."

Ignoring the sarcasm, I was still hesitant on how I would answer the question. How could I possibly tell this very successful attorney I sell my goodies by day and strip at night? Although my occupation did not define me as a person, not everyone was that understanding of the situation.

Luckily, I was saved by the knock at the door. "Room service" a lady spoke very softly. Marcel removed my feet from his lap to answer as I laid on the bed, still trying to figure out how to get around the question of my job. I knew eventually he would ask again.

As the attendant pushed in the cart full of goodies, I could not help but notice the plate of fruit with a side of whipped cream, wine on ice, and a plate covered so I could not see what was on it. He was obviously full of surprises and I was taking in every minute of it. He gave her a tip and closed the door as she exited the room. I was feeling so good inside. So far, the night was all

I expected and more. He poured both of us a glass of wine. "A toast to new beginnings", he said jokingly as we both laughed.

Anxious to know what was on the plate, I walked over to the cart and removed the covering. My mouth instantly began to water when I saw the T-bone steak, loaded baked potato, and mixed vegetables. Now I understood why there was only one plate. It was enough for the both of us.

After taking another sip of wine, I sat my glass down and began to seduce him. Removing my dress, I let it fall to the floor revealing nothing underneath. He was speechless. I twirled around to show him some of my stripper moves, attempting not to look too professional. He watched for about ten minutes until he could no longer deal with the teasing, pulling me down to the bed and kissing me all over as he began to undress. My body was filled with excitement. And afterwards, we fell asleep in each other's arms.

Chapter 13

  The next morning, I was awakened by the bright sun shining through the window, realizing I was alone. It was almost noon and Marcel was nowhere in sight as I laid in a stranger's bed completely unclothed. Although I consumed a decent amount of alcohol, I recalled the night clearly. In that moment, I felt wanted; just to awaken to the reminder of the whore whom I really had become. Never any shame in my actions, I quickly found my clothes lying on the floor next to the bed and began to dress as I would after any other services performed. Unbothered by the crust in my eyes, I grabbed my purse and exited the room, hurriedly down the hallway before anyone could see me.

Arriving back in my room, I checked my cell phone. As expected, not one missed call. As much as I was used to not having any friends or family, for some reason a feel of loneliness came over me. Becoming so isolated from the world, I pushed away everyone who attempted to care for me, ashamed of the judgement they would pass upon my activities. Or maybe it was the fact of me not wanting to hear of the truth about who I had really become. My eyes began to water as I sat on the edge of my bed, starring at myself in the mirror. This trip was intended to free me from the bondage I was feeling back in Tampa, yet, once again, I was in a compromising situation, allowing my insecure brokenness to order my steps. No matter where I would go, my past followed, and I was controlled by the lifestyle I adopted. It made me question self, whether I knew who I really was.

Drying my tears with the back of my hands, I decided to take a long bubble bath, soaking in the darkness with just me and my thoughts. Maybe visiting my father was not such a bad idea. It would give me a sense of closure and exonerate some of the pain I was allowing to consume me. Any other day I would absorb myself into work, ignoring the reality of the things that were really taking place. As crazy as it sounded, my work was my haven, providing an escape from the realities of my upbringing. I did not have to think about death, nor all the terrible things that took place in my life. Sex with random men gave me the feeling of empowerment, being the only thing in my life I could control.

After soaking for over an hour, I made the decision to right some of my wrongs by going to visit my father. Things between us were never well. The only thing I could recall was him telling me I was going to end up just like my mother if I did not change my ways. Of course, in my adolescent mind, I thought he meant committing suicide. But even I knew I had so much more to live for to even consider the idea. Yet, he was speaking of her dysfunctional ways, the lack of affection and love I neglected to give, the inconsideration of others, and most importantly, failure to nurture my own child. I was numb inside just as my mother once was, continuing a life of self-destruction. The only difference, I no longer suffered through poverty. Climbing up the ladder in my idea of success, I lacked nothing. Anything my heart desired I could provide it without having to ask of someone else. I lived in the suburbs with a car that was paid for and my bank account was very hefty if I had to say so myself. It was true, everyone had their problems, but not everyone was afforded the opportunity to live a life of luxury while enduring them. They said money could not buy everything, but I was one lucky woman to have experienced so many of life's trials and tribulations and finally live a life of comfort. Who cared how the money was made…if I continued to make it?

I decided to look my best for the visit. After all, it had been years since daddy laid eyes on me. My anticipation was for him to see me and realize how wrong he was, for him to say how proud he was of me and no longer look at me as the juvenile delinquent he could not wait to be rid of. I took a second look in the mirror, pleased with my selection of clothing. Grabbing my purse, I confidently walked out of my hotel room towards the elevator.

With over a two-hour drive to Jackson Heights, I blasted my music as I drove towards the I-787 south ramp. According to my GPS, there was one hundred fifty-four miles to look forward to. There was no way I could have taken an Uber; however, I never had any problems with road trips.

As I continued, my mind began to take me back to those years spent with Justin. I wondered if he was still around and if so, would he have recognized me. Around that time, he would have been in his early forties, maybe settled with a few kids. I smirked at the idea. Some people never change no matter how old they may get in age. I could still picture him hanging around the city, collecting from his young workers then going home to pop pills and smoke his weed. He was my first for everything, sex, drugs, money; I was so taken by his hustle and how he operated. The only difference between he and I, he never wanted more out of life. He was content with the empire he built, never expecting for it to crumble. But then again, some people operate without a conscious. He never cared if lives were lost nor if families suffered. In a way, that was my story as well, except for the part where people had to die. Sure, I may have ruined a couple of families. Having sex with married men is not something very ethical and I always considered the damage that could be done if my client's wives were to find out about me. We are all dysfunctional in some sort of way, not one person being better than the other. My sinful ways were no worse than the next, so why did I feel so condemned by others?

As I pulled up to the last known address of my father and stepmother, it crossed my mind to wonder if anyone still lived here. Although I did not realize it back then, my dad must have made a decent living to provide such a nice sized home in the city. The houses there were much more than I was willing to pay, even in today's economy. Even the least expensive home was above my price range and I never understood why everyone had to live so close together. Maybe it was a possibility that my dad sold drugs as well. How else could he afford a million-dollar home?

I sat in the car just looking at the house I spent my teenage years living in. It was the same as I remembered it, red brick, three stories, with the iron burglar bars on the front door. There was a red awning coving the front porch, with a set of chairs I had never seen before. I slowly exited my vehicle and walked up the sidewalk towards the front door. But what I was about to discover was of nothing what I expected. A very young and handsome Caucasian man opened the front door, looking at me as though I must have been lost. He was holding a glass of something and chewing as though he was in the middle of a meal. He must have spotted me approaching through the open window. Checking the numbers on the house, ensuring I was at the correct address, I became dumbfounded.

"May I help you with something?", the gentleman asked. He seemed to be just as confused as I was.

I stopped on the sidewalk, afraid to approach any closer. "I'm looking for Mr. and Mrs. Matthews. I was convinced I had the correct address." Thinking in my head, I should have confirmed if they still lived there before driving for nothing. How naïve of me to have believed they would reach out in the event of moving considering I never responded to the message Dana left on my Facebook page months ago. She said my dad had taken sick, but she never mentioned how sick. I guess it was up to me to call and find out. But I became so consumed with work, it completely slipped my mind.

"You must be talking about the older couple who lived here previously. I just purchased this home two months ago. But according to my realtor, the previous owners passed away."

My heart dropped. A part of me wanted to eliminate the idea of it being my father and step mother whom he was speaking of, but when he went back in the house, returning with an old blanket I watched Dana spend hours crocheting, the tears began to stream down my face. My heart broken in more than two pieces; I could not take any more heartache. Why was this happening to me? How much pain could one person endure in one lifetime?

"I found this down in the basement. Maybe you would like to have it."

My body was numb and stiff. I could not move. I just wanted to go home. And not to the hotel home, but back to Tampa to crawl into bed and never leave. He must have understood what I was feeling. Walking over to hand me the finished blanket, he murmured, "I'm so sorry for your loss." I reached out my arms to receive what was left of them, hoping it was all another dream. But it wasn't. The man turned to walk back into his home, leaving me there to deal with my emotions all alone.

BOOK TWO

The Discovery of Corrie Matthews

Chapter 14

For He knoweth our frame; He remembereth that we are dust.

Psalm 103:14 KJV

Do you believe there is truly a purpose for everyone's life, no matter how damaged it may appear? I asked myself this question over and over on my flight home from New York. It seemed no matter where I turned, nothing but unwelcoming news followed. For two weeks I prayed, I meditated, and I prayed some more, taking my discoveries in New York as a sign that God had been calling my name, ignoring every one of His requests and leaning into my own understanding and guidance.

Lost in a world of confusion, the enemy had taken over and I felt defeated. After days of unpacking and reevaluating my life, I finally decided to talk to Nick. As expected, he picked up on the first ring.

"Do you believe in God?" I could hear him breathing on the other end of the phone but no response. It became so silent, I thought maybe he hung up. "Nick, why won't you answer me?"

"Because no one has ever asked me that question before. But yeah, I mean…. I believe there is a higher power than us. How else would we all exist?" Honest, yet confused by where all of this was coming from, he attempted to answer the question in an intellectual way that would make him sound as though he possessed some sort of religious background, but the truth of the matter still existed that neither of us knew anything; not because we did not want to but because of our ignorance of the scriptures.

"Where is all of this coming from Co? Don't tell me you went up north and your dad turned you all religious on me." He laughed before pausing to listen to the weakly sobbing on the other end. I could not contain my composure as my cries grew louder and louder. "I'm on my way over Corrie. And don't tell me it's nothing." Listening on the other end as he grabbed his keys, I heard a loud slam, a front door closing, and then another, sounding like a car door. He started the engine and I continued to hold patiently as the roaring of his motor let me know he was in route. I grasped the phone tightly in my palm, pressed against my ear firmly, listening to every sound to come through so I could determine his destination. Tears continued to roll down my cheeks as my eyes watered beyond my control. Depression and guilt were slowly beginning to consume me as flash backs of my mother's suicide took control of my thoughts. It seemed easier to check out of this world of uncertainty rather than to deal with the afflictions of life that we tend to experience.

When I no longer could hear the music from the radio, I knew Nick was now in the driveway and I began to walk towards the front door, unlocking it to let him in. Once inside, we both ended the call on our cell phones and welcomed one another with a tight embrace which lasted for over sixty seconds. Not yet ready to discuss what had taken place, I just wanted to be in Nick's presence. I still loved and cared for him deeply and no matter how hard I tried to let go, I needed him around.

"How was your trip baby girl? Everything ok?" Attempting to fight back the tears, I glanced at him through my glaring eyes, shaking my head to indicate things were not alright. I was in pain, in a serious state of depression, fighting to regain my sanity and a sense of normality but I did not know how to express these feelings without the excessive crying. He pulled me close to him to allow for me to let it out as he embraced me tightly in his arms.

I remembered as a little girl, reading something about how God never puts more on you than you could handle. But what did that really mean? With all the heartache, trials and tribulations I faced, I was certain to have been one of the few who was not included in that ratio. Having dealt with some challenges that should have knocked me on my bottom by now, I sometimes could not believe how fortunate I was to remain among the living when thinking about incidents from my past. My entire family had been taken away from me, and yet, I was still here, alive and well to tell my story. Although that should have been more than enough to be thankful for, the tragedies kept occurring, causing me to feel punished and unfavorable.

Crying myself weary, a sense of sleepiness came over me. Placing my legs on the sofa, I laid my head in Nick's lap and began to close my eyes. Even after the disagreement, which transpired before I left, there was something about having him there that made me feel relaxed and secure. He must have been feeling the same way because minutes later he was falling asleep as well.

Hours went by before waking up to pitch black darkness, looking up to notice the whites of Nick's eyes staring down at me. I sat up to turn on the lamp. "You hungry?", he asked, never taking his eyes off me.

"Yeah but I don't really feel like going anywhere. Takeout?" He smiled, nodding his head in agreement. I knew he wanted to talk. Not only about what happened in New York, but to finish the conversation we began before I left. Unsure of which subject I was ready to tackle first, I blurted it out. "My dad died.", fighting back the emotions that were attempting to come out with it. Never wanting to play the victim, it was something about allowing people to feel sorry for me, or as my therapist would refer to it, being empathetic. It caused me to feel less independent and more vulnerable. Who cared about how I was feeling when there were so many other problems and concerns to deal with? Why stop everything you are doing just to be a shoulder for someone else to cry on? Had I really become that cold and disconnected from life?

Zoned out into deep thought, I could see Nick's mouth moving, realizing he was responding to what I just confided in him. "Co, are you listening to me? Maybe you should seek some professional help to get you through all of this because I hate to see you hurting baby girl. Let's be real about the situation. You are popping pills, smoking weed, and selling your body. How is that helping you fix what you are feeling inside? And then you are avoiding an even bigger issue you are facing. You are in denial, but I see straight through you."

"I have been seeing someone off and on but it's not enough. I need more. Something's missing Nick." Once again, I began to cry heavily. I was hurting, and the pain cut deeply, but I could not put my finger on the cure. I lost my happiness, or maybe I never found it.

Chapter 15

Nick and I talked for hours. He even slept over, and for the very first time, we stayed in different bedrooms. Knowing we could never be together in the way I pictured it, my feelings for him remained the same. I loved him without ceasing and desired for him to continue to be a part of my life.

Thinking back on when I was younger, I never wanted my life to become as dysfunctional as those who influenced me the most. Yet, there were no other relationships to base my guidance other than the broken ones I descended from. It was a cycle I became more determined to break.

I was the first one out of bed. After washing my face and brushing my teeth, I decided to make Nick and myself some breakfast. As I began the preparations, pulling out the carton of eggs and pack of bacon from the refrigerator, I contemplated on how life would have been if we were together and he was not married, and how it would be living a normal life with a regular nine to five. He would help me raise Vanessa and I would rise every morning before everyone else to start breakfast.

"What are you smiling so brightly about this morning? I thought we slept in different rooms."

His sarcasm was cute, but I knew he really wanted me next to him last night. Nick was standing in the kitchen doorway in some jogging pants and no shirt. The ripples of his abs were seducing me to come and get what I was missing while in the back of my mind I was telling myself to look away. Yet, I could not help but notice a look of discouragement on his face.

"I hope you're hungry." I smiled while looking down into the kitchen sink in search of a bowl to scramble the eggs. My desire for him was obvious but he was never the type to take advantage of my vulnerability. My 'no' usually meant take me now, and my 'stops' were an indication of how badly I really wanted him. He knew how to read my body language and was the only one to make me weak at the knees. But I only needed him to be a friend at that moment.

"Co, Leslie and I are getting divorced." Sounding disappointed and frustrated, I was fighting to hide the joy I wanted to feel about the astonishing news. Praise God and hallelujah was what I wanted to yell, but I knew now was not the time to convert to my naturally selfish ways. Nick needed me to listen as he done the night before. I pulled up a stool from the bar to sit and give him my undivided attention. He was still standing, leaning against the wall, looking down at the floor.

"I know this is a lot. But I also know you are a very strong woman and I was thinking this could be our chance to see if we could be together. If I can get out of the drug game, then I know you are more than capable of making a change as well. It seems you want to, otherwise, you would not have called me to ask the question you asked. Something is going on up there in that head of yours."

Eager to do what was right, I wanted to be able to give up everything for a more abundant life of honesty and good. But my lack of trust would not allow it. I could only live by what my eyes could see and what I knew to be true. If I gave up my work, who would take care of me? How would my bills get paid? And most importantly, how would I survive? Everything I knew depended on my hustle. If the money stopped, my empire would crumble, leaving me with nothing.

Knowing my stubbornness, Nick gave up on trying to get through to me. We ate breakfast in silence. Trying not to think too much into it, I zoned out, attempting to not allow for my emotions to get the best of me. Loving Nick was one thing but believing we could be together was farfetched from the reality of it all.

Chapter 16

"I don't know where it all began. I was always left alone, never anyone around but strange adults and other kids my age, female and male of many different walks of life. My memory is clouded. Maybe it is from the excessive amount of weed I smoke." I began to chuckle to ward off the crying. As much as I refrained from allowing my thoughts to take me to those dark places, I knew then was the time to let go and put it all to rest. Dr. Hunt sat across from me, engaged in what I was saying while observing my body language and documenting her feedback.

"The clearer recollections of my life are of the things that hurt me the worse." I leaned forward in my chair, looking down at the ground, remembering when I was seven. "My mom was at work and my brother and I were home alone. Only months away from turning sixteen, he was old enough to stay at home to babysit me. He invited a few of his friends over to play video games, knowing my mother would not be home until late in the evening. I sat on my bed, playing with my dolls and listening to the chaos going on in the other bedroom, overhearing my brother telling one of his friends, 'once my little sister falls asleep, we can head out'. I knew what that meant but convinced myself he would never leave me that late at night by myself. I had been locked out on several occasions and ended up sleeping at a friend's house until my mom could leave work and take me home, but never was I unattended. He turned the lights off and locked both the front and back door, but he didn't check to make sure everyone had left. One of his friends was still in the bathroom, and instead of letting himself out, he came into the room I was in. I remember closing my eyes tightly, wanting him to leave. I thought, if he thinks I am sleeping, he wouldn't want to wake me, or I'll scream or something like that, but he didn't. He pulled the covers back, slowly rubbing his hand up my night gown before pulling my panties down to my ankles… and…." I was sobbing, wanting to tell the story exactly how it took place. "I remember… the… the feeling of his finger going inside me. I tried to clinch but he grabbed my leg with his other hand, holding me down with his upper body so I could not move. Feeling overpowered, I just laid there, no longer putting up a struggle. Crying harder, attempting to catch my breath through every sentence, "it hurt!", I yelled through the sniffling. I felt as though it was happening all over again, and I could feel the sharp pains inside of me. As I cried, Dr. Hunt handed me a second box of tissues.

I was wrong about my destiny and I made things harder on myself, both knowing and unknowing. The life choices I made caused me to suffer, but nothing about that day was my fault. Maybe the poor parenting and mishaps of my life shaped me into the person I became. The demons of fear took over me and I lacked the motherly instinct, not wanting to destroy Vanessa's life as badly as my own mother destroyed mine.

Releasing a deep sigh, I began to take in what Dr. Hunt was saying. "You cannot change the things that have happened to you in your past nor can you erase the pain, but you can strive for better. You can create stability and a healthier life for you. You must let go and move forward. Do not waddle in misery or blame yourself for the mistakes your parents made. Make a change so you and your daughter can have a better future. Be a page turner. I would like for you to journal about your day to day feelings and bring it to your next session." She smiled, creating hope for brighter days. I knew she was right, and I wanted to believe it. The only thing stopping me was the idea of not knowing how I could survive making less money.

At the end of my session, as I was walking to my car, my cell phone began to ring. Digging deep inside my designer purse, I finally located the rectangular device underneath the depth of my other belongings. A 404-area code appears on the screen, but I had no idea who it could be. Reluctantly, I answered to a voice on the other end that I never thought I would hear again in my lifetime.

"Good afternoon gorgeous, I hope I'm not interrupting anything." Not having to say his name, I automatically recognized Marcel's voice on the other end. Smiling from ear to ear, I was at a loss for words. We never spoke again after our one-night stand in New York. He was already gone when I woke up in his bed and after arriving back to the hotel from finding out about my dad, I immediately packed my things and checked out. I left so suddenly that I did not have the opportunity to leave him my number, which was even more flattering to the idea of him calling.

"How did you get my number?", I asked, both flattered and curious at the same time.

"I hope you don't mind, but we attorney's do have a way with obtaining information when we really want it." He laughed which made me begin to laugh as well. Unsure of it being a good or creepy thing to do, I was very impressed by the idea of this man taking the time out to get in contact with me. For some reason it made me feel wanted and desired.

"No, I don't mind at all. It's good to hear from you. How have you been?" I was sitting in my car with the key in the ignition but in no hurry to move. He had me mesmerized and blushing like I never blushed before, wanting our conversation to carry on for as long as possible. Once feeling like he could see past nothing more than what was between my legs, I understood what it felt like to have a man show true interest in me. He wanted to know everything that was going on since we last saw one another and before I knew it, he was asking if it was possible for him to fly down for a visit. "Staying in a hotel wouldn't be a problem. I don't want you to think I only want to come for one reason. I just want to spend more time with you to really get to know who you are as a person." Not believing what my ears were hearing, I quickly accepted, eager to see where this friendship could possibly take us. My memory reverted to the night we shared, remembering clearly how I was the one to seduce him. I began to wonder what would have happened if I never came on to him. Would he have been eager to have sex with me or would we have talked all night, just to eventually fall asleep in one another's arms?

Not wanting to get my hopes up for disappointed, I quickly snapped out of my what if's. After all, nothing good ever happened in my life and I would be naïve to really expect things to change now. Even if things were to work out between Marcel and I, it was only a matter of time before I would find a way to mess it all up. Not only that, I was yet to tell him about the field of work I worked in, certain he would run the other way once he realized he was pursuing a prostitute the entire time.

"So how about two weekends from now? Can you clear your schedule for an old friend?" His determination was persistent. Wishing there was a way to see one another before then, I decided two weeks would be enough time for me to get my life together, so he could not see how dysfunctional I really was. I also needed to come up with an itinerary for an entire weekend that was not structured around sexual activities. For once in my life, my thoughts had to expand beyond what I was used to and into a dimension of really beginning to understand other aspects of getting to know a person. Not only did I accept the challenge, but I accepted the possibilities that came with it. Marcel and I connected for a few more minutes before ending the call. Afterwards, I programmed his number into my phone and drove out of the parking lot. My next stop had to be Deslyn's house.

I drove for miles, giving me time to clear my thoughts. She lived on the other side of town in Clearwater, closer to the beaches and away from the environment of the club. When I pulled up to her house, I parked in the driveway behind her black on black 2019 Range Rover. Always admiring her taste of style, I often sought to one day be just like her, but that all changed after she was facing many federal charges and losing everything. The last I heard, Deslyn was in the negative and possibly seeking to file bankruptcy to prevent her from being out on the streets. The club was now up for sale and an auction was scheduled to take place on her seven thousand square foot house thirty days later. She was in a tough situation and I was visiting to see if there was any assistance I could offer.

Not calling to inform her of my arrival, I began to ring the doorbell in hopes of someone being inside. After standing on the porch for over five minutes, Des finally answered the door. Her hair was a mess and she was wrapped in a champagne colored silk robe in the middle of the afternoon. If things could not be any worse, she reeked of alcohol. Looking surprised that anyone would take the time out to visit, she welcomed me inside with a tight embrace. We walked through the foyer, past both the living room and dining area, which both appeared half empty, and into her downstairs home office. She took a seat in the leather chair behind her hand carved, rustic office desk as I sat on the chase lounge in the corner, overlooking the view of her pool in the backyard. We both sat silently, taking in the reality of everything that took place over those past few weeks.

"How are you holding up?", I asked with my deepest of sympathy. If anyone knew how it felt when life handed you lemons, it was me. With all I experienced in life, I was prepared to give her some words of encouragement.

"You know why I chose you Co?" She began to reminisce on when we first met. "You were a cute little girl, lost and in need of guidance. I knew you were clueless to who I was nor did you know what I was. But I trusted you enough to take you in and nurture you, take care of you, and provide you with the things no one else would. The club was truly no environment for someone like yourself, but you made me a lot of money and it was a way for me to protect you from the outside world." Though I felt like I was getting a drunken lecture from a parent, I continued to sit and listen. Des was my role model whom I looked up to, a person I envied and wanted to replicate in the future. I was young, and not knowing any better, I followed in her footsteps. Never telling her what I did on the side, I was ashamed she would look down on me as she did her street workers. Yes, I was a dancer, but I carried myself as someone who could have more in life, who wanted to be more, and dancing was only a temporary financial resource to my master plan at work. I knew it did not define me, nor was it God's plan for my life.

"The club is closing for good and it is time for you to venture off to do your own thing. I'm too old to continue this life I have been living and I am finally at a point where I can give it up. I'm thankful for the side hustle which allowed for me to stash some funds in my private safe where no one could find. I'm not fighting the IRS, it's not worth it. I have relinquished everything, and we were able to come to an agreement. Once the house sales I will return to my home in the Dominican to be with my family. Co, this life is never meant to be forever."

The words she was speaking to me at that moment were breathing life into my doubts. Never had she spoken so positively about my future. Focused on making a quick dollar, I did not look ahead to see the end of the road I was on. I could not see a life without the club nor could I see Deslyn humbling herself to the point of full submission. Now that I was being honest with myself, I wanted this lifestyle to be forever, never planning a different route or considering different ventures and opportunities. I was forced to think outside of the box, which seemed a lot larger than the insulated space I confined myself to for many years.

"Des, I just want to thank you for all you have done, not only for me, but for all the other girls you extended an opportunity to. Many people would not look at it as something to be proud of, but this chapter in my life has shown me that I am more than capable of rebuilding a life different from what I am accustomed to."

Deslyn's optimism was inspiring. Driving over, I was expecting her to feel hopeless and abandoned, and yet, she inspired me to think positively about the endless possibilities which were ahead, considering Duchess was no more. She showed me that, no matter what the circumstances may look like, the outcome was endless, and I must believe there was more to life. Everything happened for a reason and the closing of the club was truly a blessing in many ways.

Later that night when I arrived home, I poured myself a glass of wine and relaxed on the couch. With all that took place in one day, I felt like I was experiencing an indirect intervention. I grabbed the blanket on the ottoman and wrapped it around my body as I began to feel relaxed. Minutes later, I dozed off into a deep sleep.

Chapter 17

I took my loss as a destruction of self, downplaying all the many endeavors I had going for myself as though my world ended. Nothing felt right. Matter of fact, it was so different, I struggled with catching up to time. It was though it abandoned me in the middle of the night. I wanted to run back, but it was much too late. My world was now moving into a different direction. In a direction of growth and opportunity. I had no choice but to leave everything else behind and move forward, allowing my thoughts to dig deeper into my inner strength and beauty.

Who am I to say life can be a little unjust and cruel? With so many others suffering all around the world from much larger issues than my own, how selfish it is of me to now be in my feelings, thinking life is unfair. Feeling neglected by those who proclaim to have love for me, boredom gravels at my thoughts. But this feeling I am having did not come about so abruptly. Oh no! This took years of buildup, selfishly investing my all into myself rather than the needs of others.

Another day closer to my freedom, yesterday is gone, tomorrow is only a dream, and today is gloomy as hell out. But thank God, I am alive. I often wonder how our destinies are predetermined and exactly how many blueprints of our lives does the Big Guy upstairs have on everyone. It is inevitable that our fate will go exactly as He has planned, no matter how stubborn or disobedient we may be at times. But once redirected, that creates another blueprint.

Never having any guarantees in life, how does one avoid hardship and anguish? We work hard to obtain a certain goal, not prepared for the downfalls that come with the territory. I for one look at fear of myself as being my largest barrier for growth. Never are we born knowing our capabilities and our expectations of life. We do not know who is meant to stay nor who is meant to go, allowing hopeful wishing as well as undeniable devastation.

I am a star in my own eyes. Often imagining how life could be so different if I could get my emotions to get on board and stop being so stubborn and lost in time. Mixed feelings, for the past few weeks, have dangled with me and will not let go. Running out of fuel, I continue to push, like an automobile trying to get to the nearest gas station, in hopes of eventually reaching my happy place.

A firm knock at the door disrupted my sleep. It was Sunday morning and barely day light out. Keeping the blanket wrapped loosely around my chilled body, I walked to the door slowly, aggravated by the unexpected visit. Anyone who knew me understood to call before popping up to my house.

As I opened the door, I noticed Tasha standing there dressed up in her Sunday morning church clothes, her purse in her left hand and a bible in her right. "Nobody knows how to use a phone anymore I see." It had been weeks since we last spoken and from what I heard; she was now working a nine to five for the city of Tampa.

Ignoring my comment, she pushed pass me, inviting herself inside. "I'm off to this new church I started attending and thought maybe you would be interested in joining me."

Still half sleep, I picked up my phone to notice it was only seven a.m. "Tasha, who goes to church this early in the morning? I'm no saint but I'm sure this is even too early for

Sunday school hours." Letting out a huge yawn, I curled back up on the sofa in hopes of her getting the hint and letting herself out. There was no way I was about to step foot in anyone's church just for those church folks to look at me like some sort of heathen, passing judgement and whispering hateful things about me behind my back. And let us not start on the preacher, who was only going to ask for different offerings the entire time.

"First of all, I got dressed early so I could come over and wait for you to get dressed. Secondly, the church is an hour away from your house. Service starts for nine thirty so if we are going to make it in time, I need for you to get up and put some clothes on." Tasha was standing over me as if she were my mother who was not taking no for an answer.

"I understand you want to save my soul but today is not that day. I am tired and getting dressed this early in the morning is just not happening. And I know there is a much later service than nine thirty. Who in the hell gets up voluntarily this early in the morning if they don't have to?" I had my fair dealings with people of the church, even danced for a few of them.

Although frustrated, she decided not to press the subject. Instead she took a seat next to me and watched quietly as I fell back to sleep. Maybe it was the closing of the club, or even other life events that caused this change to take place in her life. But then again, who was I to say it was not who she was from the beginning? She never confided in me and I could not name one time where I saw her dancing or up on the poll. I was beginning to think she was a secret spy, maybe even an agent. I wondered if she ratted on Des, deciding it was my turn to pick her brain for answers.

"Hey Tash", I began to mumble from under the covers, expecting she could hear me.

"Yeah."

"Are you a secret detective or maybe a Jehovah's Witness or something?" I then began to laugh at the thought of her being dressed as a nun.

"Corrie, why would you think I'm a Jehovah's Witness? There is nothing wrong with going to church. You would think with all that has happened in your life, maybe something would spark an urge for you to get your life right with God." There was frustration in her tone and her voice began to rise. "You ever consider how it is not normal to isolate yourself from the world as if you don't need anyone? Or maybe how selfish it is for you to disregard the fact that there is a little girl who yearns for a mother, but you are too cold hearted to acknowledge you even have a daughter. There is not enough money and designer logos in the world to cover up your disfunctions. Do you really think your fancy clothes and expensive cars are going to get you into heaven? Do you really think God cares about how much money you made over the years from taking your clothes off for strangers? And here I am trying to be a friend and help you find your way back to reality, but you are too screwed up in the head to realize it." Tasha grabbed her things and stormed out, slamming the door behind her.

At a loss for words, there was a feeling of guilt that took over me. Although I was joking, I let my feelings get the best of me and pushed away someone who was only trying to help, but at the same time, could not believe she just had the balls to go off on me in my own house.

Picking up my phone, I began to dial Tasha's number in hopes she had not traveled too far and maybe she could have a little mercy towards my ignorance. When she answered on the second ring, I became grateful for a second chance.

"I'm really sorry. Can you come back?" The first time ever showing remorse for pushing someone away, it felt good to apologize and even better to know she forgave me. Tasha immediately turned around. I knew I hurt her feelings and that she was honestly trying to be a friend.

Walking back through the door I failed to lock, I could not help but notice the bible she walked out with still in her hand. "I want you to have this", she said as she handed it to me. Unmoved by the gesture, I took it, so we could move forward.

"You know I'm still not going to church with you right?" We both smiled. Although she could not win this argument, the battle had just begun.

Chapter 18

I find then a law, that, when I would do good, evil is present with me. For I delight in the law of God after the inward man: But I see another law in my members, warning against the law of my mind, and bringing me into captivity to the law of sin which is in my members.

Romans 7:21-23 KJV

Two weeks passed, and it was the day of Marcel's arrival. I woke up early to clean and to also make sure I was looking my best. With the club closing, my schedule became more flexible, allowing more availability for me to book clients at the spa throughout the week and leave my weekends open for whatever I choose.

Watching the clock so I knew to leave at a descent time, I double checked myself in the mirror and packed a, just in case bag, for the possibility of staying the night at his hotel room. Although that was not the plan, I wanted to be prepared for everything.

As I pulled up to the airport, my phone started to ring. Answering through the speaker function of my car, he tells me that he is out front waiting. Wearing some khaki shorts with a superman tee, he immediately reached out for a hug, squeezing me tightly before putting his luggage in the trunk of my car. He was looking and smelling exactly how I remembered. We drove around the city, sightseeing and admiring all of God's creation, stopping at Joe's crab shack for lunch. He opened the door for me everywhere we went and was a complete gentleman the entire time. After lunch, he wanted to book his room. There was a Westin close by, so he decided to book there. I waited in the car until he came out with the room key, in case someone whom may have recognized me was inside the lobby.

Once inside, I made myself comfortable on the bed. "Are you going to make us a drink?", I reached in my purse to pull out a cigar packet which housed the piece of joint I was smoking on earlier that morning. As I reach for my lighter, I hear Marcel, in a shocking tone, "what do you think you're doing?" I looked up to notice him standing directly in front of me holding two drinks but looking down at what was in my hand. "Corrie, I don't do drugs and you can't have that around me, so I would appreciate if you would not do that in the presence of my company." Not knowing if he were serious or not, I shrugged my shoulders and put it away. Accepting my drink from his hand, I drank half of it down, not wanting to deal with the embarrassment of what just happened. Neither of us said anything else about it. Instead, he grabbed my hand and led me to the bed, gesturing for me to lay down for a back massage. As I climbed onto the bed, I laid on my stomach, not bothering to remove the knee-high sundress I had worn.

For almost an hour I was the client, rather than the worker. I was the one getting special treatments and relaxing to the touch of someone else's hands. As much as I wanted to show Marcel my skills as well, telling him about my professional occupation may not have went well with the occasion. He may not have been as accepting as I would want him to be and running off a man of his position would have been foolish of me, especially considering the jerks I met over the years. True enough, I did not know him well enough to say he was as sincere as he appeared, but I was liking what he was throwing. I wanted to experience a man who catered to me and knew how to treat a woman with respect and loyalty. Maybe Marcel wasn't that man, but I could pretend, even if it was just for this one night.

After my massage, he and I laid there in the bed, him holding me closely to his chest, in silence. It felt like being in one of those movies, the ones when they look in love. The awkward silence was making me feel uncomfortable and I needed to say something, but I had no clue how to start a conversation with such a wordy individual. His level of intellect was impressive, and I knew he expected a woman who was at lease somewhere on his level.

I began to think about the time I met the gentleman at the rest stop when I first moved to Florida. He seemed to have the same professional charisma about himself, confident about what he wanted, and seeking after it until the deal was closed. I wanted that man in my life, showing me what it was like to experience true, unconditional love, and going through the rough patches with me without growing weary of what the future may bring. But that would never happen because my heart was guarded, and I was afraid of trusting another with something so fragile to me. I experienced heartbreak like nonothers and went through some tough losses. Although it made me stronger, it also made me aware of my tolerance for heartache. I chose to be alone so that I never would experience loss again.

Not realizing it, Marcel had fallen asleep. I closed my eyes in an anticipation of catching up but as usual, my thoughts would not let me rest. I tried counting something, but I couldn't even think of what to count. I began to rub my free hand along the groves of Marcel's muscular chest, slowly and softly, around his shoulder and up and down his arm that was not holding me. With no intentions of waking him. My intentions were never to go to a hotel to sleep. But as I laid there I realized, I was using sex as a way of feeling my emptiness, as a way of receiving attention, and what was even more disturbing, it was my only way of expressing love. Marcel grabbed my hand before I could continue exploring the rest of his body. "Why don't we just lay and enjoy one another's company. It's not always about sex." The first time any man ever turned me down, I felt rejection rather than appreciated. "I think that I'm going to go back to my place now.", I say to Marcel as I slid from underneath the sheets, still fully clothed.

"What do you mean? Because I refuse to have sex with you, you're refusing to stay? So, is that all this is about?" Marcel seemed livid. "Corrie, I didn't come all of this way just for you to come have sex with me at a hotel room. There are plenty of women in my hometown who would love, given the opportunity, to come over and do what you are trying to do." I felt everything in me begin to change as I was taking in every word that was coming out of his mouth. Did he just say that to me? Moving even faster to get all my belongings together so I could get the hell out of that room, I tried to avoid saying what I was thinking at the time. I knew I could be a firecracker when rubbed the wrong way, with very low tolerance for any off the wall comments. It was evident I was not ready for whatever it was Marcel was pursuing and I needed to leave.

Following behind me with every step, I turned around before opening the door, "I'm sorry but I can't do this." He was speechless. Not one word was spoken from his mouth and no expression of emotion concealed his face. With nothing left to be said, he did not bother to put up a fuss, instead, he let me go with the understanding he may never see me again and once again, I was walking out on love.

Chapter 19

No one could ever realize, nor could they understand the unbearable circumstances of another individual. Just because everything seems to look alright on the surface, we can be dying on the inside, screaming for help with an eagerness to belong, feeling inadequate. I was buried in confusion, wanting to feel important, but realizing I spent most of my life pushing people away.

Leaving the hotel, I had no idea where I would go nor what I was going to do. I was having a feeling of insufficiency and needed to get back into my comfort zone. I drove to the shop, uncertain of my intentions once I arrived. Should I just drive back home? What just happened? As dozens of thoughts tormented my mind, as always, I began to wonder who I really was, questioning my identity, but it went much further. I was now questioning my existence. Had I really convinced myself to believe there was nothing wrong with me when it showed in all my actions?

Deep into my thoughts, my phone began to ring. Marcel was calling, and I was sure he wanted an explanation. I ignored the call, as I was having a moment and needed to fall back from him. Afraid he would never understand the woman whom I truly was, allowing him to get close to me would only make matters worse. I was toxic to his life, a distraction from his reality, being set up for destruction.

 My selfishness could never understand the part about him traveling all this way just to see me, and yet, I found a reason to run away, leaving the scene as though I was some sort of victim. I found myself having an emotional debate, but only one person was participating… me. Do I turn around and humble myself enough to apologize for what just happened or should I call him back and tell him it was not going to work out? Decisions… decisions… and I was the worse when it came to having to make them.

Sitting in my car under the parking lot light, I was staring at the building which held the secrets to all my hidden agendas, my deepest desires, and biggest fears. In that building I let loose and became a woman of self-destruction, a woman who no longer cared. As I fell into deep, profound thoughts, my phone began to ring once more. Looking at the caller I.D on the dashboard, it was Marcel calling again. There I was, sitting at a crossroad between a man who wanted to get to know me and an occupation where men did nothing but use my body for their own personal pleasures. Yet, I was accustomed to the dysfunctional routine of my daily living. Giving it another shot, I decided to answer.

"Hey!", I try to sound unbothered, but deep down I knew I was wrong and there was no excuse for my behavior. Yet, still too stubborn to admit it, I allowed for him to lead the conversation.

"Corrie what's up with you? Did I do something wrong?" He was full of so many questions and I could not answer any of them. Afraid of commitment, along with everything else that came with the territory, I did not know how to be what he was looking for, never taking into consideration how I was overthinking the entire situation. Never once did he mention anything about a relationship and yet, there I was, running from something that was not established. All I knew was sex and it was difficult for me to gravitate to anything different. So why did he not want it? My heart was beginning to feel things that I did not want to feel.

"I think I just froze up and needed to get some air. All of this seems like it is moving too fast for me.", attempting to tell him what I was really thinking without sounding unremorseful. I seemed to have a nonchalant attitude when it came to my emotions. Never one to know how to use them, I found it easy to just leave them off.

After a few seconds of silence, Marcel decided it to be best if he returned home on the earliest flight he could catch. Nonobjective to his suggestion, I told him to have a safe flight and disconnected the call as another was coming through. Unable to recognize the number, I let the voicemail catch it to see if they would leave a message, but whomever it was didn't. Instead, the same number began to call for a second time. I let it ring, uncertain of who would call me that time of night. Could someone have seen me sitting in front of the shop? I laid my seat back and began to light the piece of joint I saved as I watched the phone number display on the screen of my stereo system. Only five minutes passed before my phone began to ring for the third time. I answered, thinking maybe it was someone with the wrong number, but when I heard the voice on the other end, anxiety took over.

He called out, "Corrie", as I sat in silence, afraid to confirm what he already knew. "Corrie, I know this is you. It's like that now? How you been beautiful?" Justin had the same voice and was on the other end of my phone, but why? It had been years since we last spoken, and I could not recall how long it had been since I saw him. There were butterflies in my stomach and a feeling of anxiety was consuming my entire body. The man who taught me everything I knew about life, about the hustle, about our ghetto version of love… was on the other end of my phone and I was unsure how I was supposed to feel about it. As if Nick and Marcel were not enough, now I was dealing with Justin, the father of my only child.

"Now is not a good time. Can I call you back?" Hurriedly to get off the phone, I hung up before he could have the opportunity to accept or decline my request. Convinced I had enough drama for one day, I decided to call it a night and drive home. Not only was I emotionally drained, my level of understanding was slowly depleting, and I was unable to grasp the concept of whether I was coming or going. I wanted to be left alone for the duration of the night, cutting my phone off to ensure there would not be any more distractions. Isolation was the key to my sanity and the temporary fix to my problems. It was easy to run away rather than face what was in front of me.

I pulled up in my driveway, eager to get out of the clothes I was still wearing from when I was with Marcel. Leaving my phone off, I was confident of a good night sleep, reassuring myself there would be no other interruptions. A person can never be to certain of their future, only knowing the happenings of the present and the occurrences of the past. I thought that to be God's way of showing me there was still rest for my kind.

After getting settled, I laid in my bed starring at the ceiling, watching the fan spin around in circles. The room was dark, light shining through the window from the outside. In my mind, my transgressions and cynical behavior finally caught up with me and I was being punished through constant grief and restraint towards life. As I laid, I was burned out, realizing my exhaustion as I cried out for rest. Although I was physically put together, emotionally and mentally I had nothing left to give. Tears began to roll down my face, not understanding the unforeseen emotions, I wondered if that was what my mom was feeling during her last hours before taking her own life. If she was anything like me, she suffered alone, not wanting the world to know her battle or see her strife with her own life. Very private and guarded from the world, I chose to fix my issues in private, minus the suicidal mentality. The challenges and setbacks taught me how to overcome all things that had been set before me. I would not fall prey to the statistics of my heritage. Although I was my mother's child, I would become the epitome of what she was not, facing my demons and fighting through the hardships until I reached my desired destination in life. Deslyn did not make me and not having the club around would not break me. I decided to no longer allow for Nick to shed a cloud of guilt over my life nor would I apologize for the lack of interest I may have shown in entertaining a monogamous relationship. I was who I was and that became enough for me.

Chapter 20

I became a sabotage to my own destiny, creating more barriers than I was able to knock down. But not even I was strong enough to stop the intentions of God. The fight was becoming too hard to defeat on my own and my heart was growing weary. I opened a door to the unknown, questioning the position of every loved one in my life and their purpose for being a part of it.

The next morning, I laid in my bed, scrolling through the newsfeed of my Facebook and checking my notifications. Questions remained of why Justin called the night before and what he could possibly have wanted. Not wanting to open another problem before closing the one's which already existed, I decided to let it go and move on with my day. There was only going to be a few more times, if any, that Marcel would allow for me to push him away before he moved on with someone else, someone who was local. I needed to decide or let him go forever. I loved the idea of being with someone, with having someone to enjoy life's teachable moments with, and give love and affection too. But an idea was all it was and all it ever would be. Not knowing how to give love nor how to receive it, I remained lost, confused, and feeling lonely. The feeling of emptiness always seemed to overbear any other feeling I could fathom. Refusing to sink into a depressive state, I reached for my phone to dial Tasha. But what would I say? Although I had given her some background on my family dynamic, I never disclosed any personal information about my life to her. The most she ever gotten out of me was about the club, but she was also the only one attempting to encourage me to go to church. I hung up the phone before she could pick up, hoping she would not call back anytime soon, at lease giving me time to think of an excuse to why I called. But as my luck would have it, she called right back. I answered after the third ring, thinking, she would only call back if I let it go to voicemail.

My heart was heavy, and I was ready to give up on everything. The temporary satisfaction from my clients was no longer doing it for me anymore and I was out of options, left to face the reality that I was really hurting deep down inside, more than a therapist could cure. No longer intrigued by the money and all the materialistic things I once focused on in life, I yearned for true happiness and stability. All it took was Tasha asking me how everything was going, and I began to break down into tears. Never crying out to anyone before, I was embarrassed but felt a release of comfort when I could hear Tasha praying on the other end of the phone. "Her life is redeemed from destruction", I continued to listen as tears rolled down my face and then I began to repeat the words I could hear coming from her mouth. "My life is redeemed from destruction! My life is redeemed from destruction!", I shouted through my tears, through my heartache, through my shame. Uncertain what would happen afterwards, I wanted to believe.

"I hear what you are saying Tash, but do you really believe this stuff?"

Pausing for a moment, she got quiet. "Corrie, I know you are not going to believe what I am getting ready to say to you. It may even freak you out to the point where you hang up in my face and never want to talk to me again. But I pray, for the sake of your soul, that you listen, and know that I am not crazy."

I sat in silence, no words to be spoken and more confused than I ever been. What could she have possibly been talking about?

"Corrie I was sent to you."

Uncertain where the conversation was going, I was full of many questions. "Huh? Sent to me how? You mean, by a family member? Do you know my family?" None of it was making any sense and I was offended by the idea of someone sending her to Florida to spy on me. It was too much for me to follow.

"Until you understand your purpose in life, you will continue your journey of confusion, allowing for the enemy to continue to devour your territory."

Who was the enemy? Was he trying to take my house? What territory was she talking about? "Tasha I am really confused, and you are making no sense to me." I wanted to know more about what she was saying.

"I have something I would like for you to try and if it does not make you feel better, I promise to fall back until you feel you are ready to discuss even further. Deal?"

"Deal." I agreed, assuming nothing she gave me could be worse than the tactics I tried already. No longer able to get through life on my own, I decided to take heed to her instructions and apply it to what I was feeling.

"I want you to read the entire book of 1 Peter in your bible. I know you have a bible because I gave it to you, but you could also download the app on your phone and read it. This is the first book I ever read when I first started reading my bible. Honestly, it was because it was one of the shortest, but in this book, I found comfort, I found peace, and it gave me a sense of encouragement knowing that God had a bigger purpose for my life. But you must be prepared to believe and receive it. Prepare your mind for what lies ahead, knowing God is in control and you too will gain a different outlook on your life."

Open to everything she was telling me, I decided to follow her instructions, still not knowing nor understanding where it would lead to. I hung up with her and spent the rest of my morning glued to the bible app I downloaded. Never considering that as a part of my daily routine, I was enjoying the quiet time, meditating on what Peter had written, until my phone began to ring. Watching as the number displayed, I noticed Justin calling again. Hesitantly, I answered.

"What's up Co! Long time no hear…how have you been?"

"Good", I mumbled through a smile to not sound bothered. The realization of him being a nonfactor in my life was overwhelmingly obvious and the only thought I was thinking to myself was, how to get him off the phone without being the Leo who I knew I could be. Besides, it would just show that he still had an advantage over my life and could still get me in my feelings, which was far from the truth.

"Did I catch you at an inconvenient time?"

Inconvenient, did he just say inconvenient? Not allowing the pettiness to take over, I replied with a subtler answer. "I was reading my bible app on my phone."

Unexpecting of the response Justin was giving, I sat, listening to the laughter on the other end, as if reading the bible was comical or something I was incapable of doing. Rather than entertaining the conversation or explaining my reason and rational, I removed myself from the conversation. In other words, I proceeded to hang up the phone without a mere goodbye. Not only did that fuel my soul but the blocking of his phone number made it even better, until he called back from a different number.

"What do you want?", I yelled to the other end.

"A place for your daughter to live."

Silence, pure silence. Before I could respond, I was crying but didn't want Justin to hear so I pulled the phone away from my ear. I did not desire to know the details, all I knew was, God was giving me a second chance to make things right with Vanessa.

> ***Finally, be ye all of one mind, having compassion one of another, love as brethren, be pitiful, be courteous.***
>
> ***1 Peter 3:8 KJV***

Chapter 21

Do you know what I have learned over time? God doesn't use perfect people. Instead, he utilizes those who are broken, tattered and worn. I have felt fear, anger, depression, and disappointment, experiencing heartbreak and rejection by others. Nothing different from anyone else's life but I remember having an epiphany, asking God when my time was going to come. His response had always been to be still. I was not ready for all He had in store. I wasn't disciplined enough, lacked focus, and was not in position to accept all He wanted to give. Never able to detour from God's plan, we are not powerful enough. However, our stubbornness can delay the process and have us wondering around in the wilderness.

In a season of building me, anything else was a distraction. My selfishness left me feeling inadequate and buried in confusion, everything the enemy wanted me to believe. But my new discovery gave me a way out.

As much as I would like to say the story ended on that day, that I got a second chance of being a mother and we lived happily ever after…it did not. Rather than things getting better, they became more difficult to bear. The faith I was slowly trying to build, with the coaching of Tasha, was being tested and the enemy was holding a very tight grip on my life.

The minute I hung up the phone from speaking with Justin, there was a very loud knock at the door. It was constant, with authority. And as I opened it, there standing in an all-black suit and tie, was a federal agent, flashing his badge and a warrant.

Apparently, my house had been under surveillance for quite some time. With reason to believe I was involved in drug possession and money laundering for Nick, they raided it without asking any questions. I sat quietly, looking over the document the officer handed me as if I knew what I was reading. Wanting to call Nick, I thought to myself, what was the point. Instead I sat in tears, thinking how my life was in shambles over a man who wasn't even mine. They went through everything, my drawers, pulling out my clothes and tossing them to the floor as if they were worthless. They destroyed my furniture, dug holes in my backyard, and seized all my jewelry as evidence. They even took the extra cash hidden in the safe.

With plans of Vanessa arriving within the next two weeks, every day leading up felt like months of torment. Not really understanding the reasons behind the sudden need to change her living arrangements, I was only grateful for a second chance, but under no circumstance was I willing to let her live with me under the given conditions. I needed to do something quickly. After hours of searching, they left, and I immediately picked up my cell phone to dial Nick, until I realized my phone may have been tapped. Grabbing my keys, I rushed to my car, seeking the nearest retail store to purchase a pre-paid throw away phone. Not even halfway out the door, I loaded the phone with minutes and attempted the call again but to my surprise, his phone was no longer in service. Standing in disbelief, I attempted a second time, same response. Unable to hold back the tears, I began to cry. Questioning God's existence was the easiest thing for me to do, as if He was a respecter of man, I assumed my temper tantrum would get His attention and make all the bad things disappear. But that's not how God operates. There was a lesson in His teachings, and He would get all glory when it was finished.

I sat in the parking lot in silence, not wanting to drive back home to the mess that had been made. The club was closed, my love life did not exist, and now I was being heavily watched by the FED's. Nick was M.I.A and I had to prepare for the arrival of a daughter whom I barely knew. Picking up my phone, I went to my bible app. If there had truly been a God like Tasha proclaimed, that would have been the time for Him to speak to me.

> ***My brethren, count it all joy when ye fall into divers' temptations; Knowing this, that the trying of your faith worketh patience. But let patience have her perfect work, that ye may be perfect and entire, wanting nothing.***
> ***James 1:2-4 KJV***

Returning to my house, I found myself in solitude, not wanting anything to do with the outside world. I cleaned as I cried and slept in between, omitting self-care and avoiding all outside communication. Not even interested in going to the spa, I asked my secretary to place a 'closed until further notice' sign in the window. My thoughts were cloudy and the only thing I could turn to that gave me comfort was my bible. As I read, I found peace and clarity. It gave me hope, knowing no matter how tarnished I felt, there was still a purpose for my life. Reading from Genesis, on to Exodus and Leviticus, I realized since the beginning of time, we were all sinners by nature. We were all created in God's image, by God, yet, still in need of a Savior. The stories were beyond what I expected, and I began to realize

I was more than what I thought I was creating. My identity had not been defined by the meaningless things I thought I needed to become somebody. My possessions could not bring me the joy I so eagerly desired. I reached for everything except for Christ. Holding on to resentment, I compared my life to others. I allowed my difficult childhood to control my way of thinking and I replaced it with things I thought would take my mind off the pain. How simple minded to believe money could buy my happiness, not realizing my emptiness until my need for comfort grew beyond my control. I was being broken down by my maker until I submitted, giving Him full control.

Chapter 22

Since the beginning of my existence, God was molding me for who He intended for me to become. Although I could not see through the heartaches and discomforts, the disappointments, and the failures, I still prevailed. I elevated myself against what the enemy meant for defeat and I pushed through to the next level. Satan wants our demise. He wants to remain in the territory he has been able to destroy for so long. He defeated my mother, and generations before her. However, despite the obstacles, I knew I was destined to be more. To sustain, we must begin to understand who we are and who we belong too. I would be lying if I said I did not consider giving up or that I have not repeatedly fallen or given in to the temptations of the flesh. I am sure they caused setbacks, but God was not done. What the enemy intended to use to destroy me, God used it to build me.

Rather than giving up and allowing my world to crumble, I fell to my knees and began to stumble over words of prayer. Unknowing of what to say, I let my heart do all the talking, crying and begging for mercy. If I knew nothing else, I knew I needed to ask for forgiveness. And as I prayed, I began repenting of everything I could think of. "Father forgive me for my deceitfulness, for my greed, for my selfishness towards others. Release me of my sexual immoralities." I could not help but think of all the inconsiderate behavior I reflected towards others. I was never pleasant. I used people for what I could get out of them, failing to appreciate those who cared for me. I prayed for discernment, and wisdom. Although my prayer was all over the place, I knew He was listening, and I could feel His presence, as if He had been waiting for me to open my eyes to this moment. It took true conviction of myself and I was still in hot water when my prayer was over. God was not letting me off that easily and Nick was good at disappearing, leaving me to take the fall for his wrong.

Two days after the search and only twelve days before my daughter's scheduled arrival, I was arrested on conspiracy to traffic. Although I knew I was innocent, they managed to take pictures of Nick leaving my house with a large amount of cash. Not only that, they were able to obtain bank records of large withdrawals from the time I took money out to give to Nick. I never asked what the money was for, but I knew it was drug related. And although I could not blame anyone but myself, the time had come for me to sit still and think about my actions. Thoughts of my conversation with Leslie flashed through my mind, realizing how I was now reaping what I had sewn. I was facing serious federal time, especially since they were unable to locate Nick, thinking I knew where he was hiding. My bail was set at ten thousand dollars, which I had no clue who I could call to post a thousand on my behalf. With no friends nor close relatives, my only hope was Tasha. The only problem was, I did not commit her number to memory. Smart phones made me so stupid; I was used to telling Siri to do whatever I asked. Noted to self, downgrade to a flip phone once I got out.

There was one number that stuck to memory, one person who I knew would not only bail me out but help me beat the case. The only dilemma, honesty. One thing I learned throughout my process; God will humble those who refuse to humble themselves. Stripped away of my entitlement, I was desperate and in need. Ready to use my only phone call, I reached out to Marcel. And surprised to hear the operator say my name, he immediately accepted the charges.

"Before you say anything or ask any questions, I just want to apologize for my behavior and the way I acted towards you. No, I'm not saying this now because I need your help, but because you are truly a genuine person and I treated you badly."

Marcel never responded to my apology. He never asked any questions, nor did he reject my request for his help. Instead, he was on the next flight to Florida to bail me out of jail and to discuss my case. I spent a total of thirty-six hours, locked up among thieves and prostitutes, and with other women who were also facing drug charges, much bigger than the one I was facing. However, we all had similar stories to tell. We all experienced difficult times, some worse than others, and we all wanted to feel loved. We needed someone who would walk with us to our purpose because I could see so much potential in all of them, which led me to reflect on my life. Why could I not see that potential in myself? Although they were facing much more time than I was, they were all encouraging me to stay positive and keep the faith. They did not allow for that dark cloud to consume their hope for a better day. I slept more peacefully that night. Although I was surrounded by strangers, I felt like I finally found people who could relate and not pass judgement on my life and how I lived for so many years.

Once released, I walked out of the building, towards Marcel's car with my head hung low. Not wanting to have the conversation I knew I would be forced to have, I refused to make eye contact. As I walked to the passenger side, he held the door open for me to get in, closing it behind me. The radio was playing Sade very softly as we drove back to my house in silence. Letting my seat back, I closed my eyes as I began to appreciate freedom and all it had to offer me. There was so much more opportunity outside of those bars called prison and I did not ever want to go back to that place again. I thought, if Marcel could get me out of the situation I gotten myself so deeply into, I would straighten up my life and live right for both, myself and my daughter. I did not want her to walk through the same, similar valleys that I endured. She was still at the age of innocence and I did not want to do anything to tarnish that image.

The car came to a complete stop. Not knowing where I lived, I was waiting for Marcel to ask for directions but instead, I was unaware of where he had taken us. Letting my seat up from its position, my heart dropped when I realized where we were parked, in the parking lot of my spa. I was speechless and embarrassed of the conversation we were about to have.

"Before you ask, know that I'm an attorney and I have the resources to obtain information on any person whom I desire. It wasn't hard to figure out what you had going on, as some of my colleagues have been some of your very loyal clients."

Taking a deep breath, I felt convicted of my sins and wanted to hide from the demons that haunted me. Knowing I would have to tell him eventually, and considering he was going to help with my case, his already knowing made it ten times worse. He reached for tissues, assuming he already knew what my reaction would be.

"Corrie I'm not judging you. I brought you here because I wanted you to see, as easily as it was for me to find out, it's going to be that much easier for the FED's to catch on about this place. You must sell, and I mean fast. They could easily persuade a jury this place is being used for drug trafficking and money laundering. And if they add prostitution to the charges, we are in for a fight to the end. I've spoken to this broker I know. From what I have already gathered, they have no surveillance on this place. Luckily, with the clients you keep, they couldn't get close enough. I must admit, I'm impressed, to say the lease, that you knew how to keep your business on the hush. Judges and politicians have inside ears and can keep them away from this place, but only for so long before they are being looked at as well. This could cause some major problems for both you and others. I'll come by tomorrow and meet him, so he can give us a ballpark-figure of how much you can get. And just so you don't alarm anyone, you need to stay as far away as possible. Agreed?"

Nodding my head, I still could not say a word. Even when I opened my mouth, nothing would come out. As grateful as I was for him assisting me, I could not fathom the idea of him conducting an extensive background check. And for him to say his colleagues were my clients, made me wonder which ones because I slept with a lot of attorneys. I decided to just keep my mouth shut for the moment, wanting to see how much information he would volunteer before I would be required to fill in the gaps. What I thought was confidential was more accessible than I imagined. I wondered how many other people knew about my lifestyle, but most importantly, had Tasha known and never said anything?

Chapter 23

Refusing to stay at my house, Marcel booked a hotel room during his stay in Tampa until the case was over. We met daily at a local coffee shop, avoiding eye contact and any other conversations off the subject of business. At times it felt uncomfortable and other times I thought about hiring someone else. However, I knew he was the only one who sincerely cared and would fight for my freedom.

Suggesting we postpone Vanessa's arrival once I expressed my concerns, he arranged for her to attend a camp somewhere in Georgia until after our court date. Justin agreed and supported my decision, which provided me with some relief. I needed to focus on getting better, so I could be a better mother for her.

From dusk to dawn, we sat at the table, him drilling me on what to expect in court and asking probing questions that I had no choice but to answer. I remember breaking down in tears, fearing the worse and feeling humiliated by my past. Detail after detail on my relationship with Nick and other situations that led to all the dismay, Marcel was getting the most intimate moments of my life. The interrogations were tormenting, having to relive my past and realizing I no longer wanted to be that person, often wondering how all of this was going to affect our relationship once it was over. My poor decisions created a mess, but the embarrassment was ten times worse than I expected. The woman who never cared about anything was now worried about everything. I never wanted to be close to anyone out of fear of one day losing them. I did not want to tear my walls down because then people would see me for the vulnerable person who I really was. I was sad, hurt and desolate all in one and as if that was not enough, I feared the opinions of others.

Every night when I got home from meeting with Marcel, I cried. Not desiring to eat nor drink anything, I took a hot bath and got into bed, laying silently in the dark until my restless body finally went to sleep. I began to lose track of time and days, cutting off all sources of communication with the outside world.

On day nine, it was obvious, and Marcel could tell my health was declining and depression had begun to set in. I was a zombie, replying to his questions in a monotone voice and sometimes only nodding my head, not wanting to speak at all. My clothes no longer matched and were wrinkled as though I did not own an iron and my hair was all over my head. Other than taking a bath and brushing my teeth, anything else was inessential to my life and the entire season became unnerving. Praying every night for it to pass, I woke up to the same depressing life I fell asleep to. The nightmare would not go away, and it became more difficult to keep it all together.

On day fourteen, while getting dressed to meet at the coffee shop as I would usually do, I was startled by a knock at the door. Hesitant to answer, I tip toed, feeling like it was the law coming to take me back to prison. But instead it was Marcel, standing there holding two cups of coffee. As I slowly opened the door, he handed me a cup and walked over to the sofa to take a seat, first taking a quick look around in observation of the house he never was invited to.

"From the way you have been showing up at the coffee shop lately, I figured I'd meet you here to save us both the embarrassment of you arriving in your pajamas." Chuckling in hopes of making me laugh, I gave him a half smile and took a seat next to him so we could get started, strongly fighting the urge to look him in the eye. I was ready for the case to be over and to face the consequences of my actions, even if it meant spending time in jail. I no longer wanted to talk about my life, about the struggles, and the things that got me to the situation I was facing.

Rather than continuing to discuss what to expect in the case, as he normally does, Marcel reached out to pull me close to him and held me in his arms. Unable to bear the pain, I sobbed quietly as tears began to soak through his navy, polo shirt. Unaware of how much I needed consoling, he held me tighter, refusing to let go and I appreciated every second. He cared enough to fight for me, for my freedom from this case and the things of this world.

"Get up. We're going for a ride." Marcel glanced at his watch as though he forgot about something and we were going to be late if we did not leave at that moment. Wanting to continue to sob in my misery, I hesitated to move. I did not like surprises. Where could he have possibly been taking me? Not giving me an option, he grabbed my keys and my purse, standing by the door until I had no choice but to join him on an unknown journey.

Once in the car, Marcel drove for approximately forty minutes before arriving to our destination. It was a shopping center with multiple businesses connected, from a Dollar General to a

Mexican restaurant. You name it, it was there. On the very end of the complex was a church and on the outside was a sign which read, welcome to prayer and worship night.

"Why are we here?", I asked irritably, remembering how thrown away I looked. My interest was not to be a part of any social gatherings during a time of distress, especially not church. Although I became very consistent in my daily bible reading, I wanted to go home and be to myself. However, ignoring my question, he grabbed me by the hand and led me to the front door where we were greeted by multiple people. Everyone was friendly and inviting, smiling as if there was no care in the world. Hugging and conversating, the foyer was consumed with fellowship and excitement to be in one another's presence. Marcel walked over to the coffee bar to make him a cup of coffee as I stood in the middle of the crowd waiting patiently.

"Hello, I'm Jessica." A friendly voice greeted me from behind and when I turned around, I could not help but notice the smiling face that went with it. "Hi, I'm Corrie."

"I haven't seen you around before. Is this your first time?"

"Yeah, I'm visiting with a friend." Drawn into the conversation, I did not want to seem rude or abrasive.

"Oh, Ok. Well, welcome! We are glad you could join us tonight for prayer and worship. I am one of the campus directors for this location. What church do you belong to?"

Embarrassed by the idea of not attending a church, I answered quietly so she would be the only one to hear me. "I actually don't have a church home at this present time."

"That's ok. You should come visit one of our Sunday services. We'd love to have you. We also have women's night once a month where us women can get together and enjoy a relaxing night away from everyday life. You should come check us out." Still smiling through every word, I wanted to experience the joy she was feeling. I could never understand how people could smile throughout life's tough circumstances when all I wanted to do was cry and be left alone.

Marcel walked up in the middle of our conversation. "Hey Jessica! It has been a long time. I see you've met my friend Corrie." Thankful he didn't refer to me as one of his clients, I smiled while nodding my head in agreeance with his statement.

"Corrie, Jessica is one of my old colleague's sister. She's the one who told me about this church, and I stopped by for the first time when I was in town a few weeks back."

Not wanting to remember it being the time I rejected him as the time he was referring to, I just kept smiling like everything was all good. He was so good to me over these last few days and I could not think of any way to repay him for his good deeds.

Just as Jessica and Marcel were deeply engaged into their conversation, a familiar face approached me, astonished by my presence. "I am so happy to see you here!" Tasha was walking towards me with extended arms ready to give me a hug. "You two know each other?", Jessica asked in amazement.

"Yes! This is the friend I was telling you about. I have been trying to get her to attend for the longest. I'm so glad she finally made it. And who is this handsome gentleman you brought with you?"

"Marcel." Surprised that I even knew anyone else in church outside of him, he extended his hand to shake Tasha's.

Music from the sanctuary rang out into the common area and everyone rushed inside like stampedes to get a seat. "You three can sit with me", Jessica exclaimed as we followed behind to where she already placed her belongings. As we entered, there was an entire band on stage playing worship music and singing to the lyrics, which were displayed on a projector like screen so the people in the congregation could sing along. Jessica and Tasha began to worship along while Marcel stood, drinking his coffee and nodding his head to the beat. I looked around throughout the crowded room, observing everyone's facial expressions, some jumping around as if we were at a live concert and others deep into the words of the lyrics being sung. And although I knew in my mind that everyone in here was battling something in their lives, it seemed this was the way for them to come alive and be set free.

Chapter 24

"I hope you enjoyed yourself. I really didn't mean to spring this on you, but it seemed like you could really use some positivity."

As Marcel spoke, I gazed out of the window while driving back to my place. I was imagining my life, more involved in church, getting to know more people, and attending functions with a family. My dreams grew into ambition and I wanted to experience a different way of living. Knowing I already burned many bridges with Marcel, I no longer considered him being the man whom I would spend the rest of my life with. I'd be lucky if he even wanted to remain friends after learning about all my skeletons in the closet.

"You hungry?" I could hear Marcel asking in the middle of my deep thoughts.

"I could definitely eat. What are you in the mood for?"

"How about you pick."

My mind immediately thought about Chinese. "I could definitely go for some shrimp fried rice and sweet and sour chicken."

"Now you're speaking my love language." Marcel smiled as he slowly placed his right hand inside of mine and squeezing it firmly but gently, reassuring me everything was going to be alright.

Getting our food to go, we arrived back to my place with anticipation of eating everything we ordered. I grabbed us some paper plates and silverware from the kitchen as he removed the food from the brown paper bag and arranged it neatly on the dining room table.

"What would you like to drink?"

"What do you have?" He asked while walking up from behind me. Startled from his unexpected approach, I jumped in dismay. "Sorry, I didn't mean to scare you." We both began to laugh as we made eye contact, quickly putting my attention back on what was inside the refrigerator and avoiding the awkwardness of things going further than they needed to. Especially since he was representing me in the court of law.

"I have water, apple juice, and white wine."

"I'll have water for now." Grabbing a bottle for the both of us, I followed him back to the table. As we sat, he reached for my hand to bless the food before starting to eat. I was amazed by the man God placed in my life. He knew exactly what I needed, when I needed it and my day was changed drastically from how it started. I did not realize how much difference it made to be surrounded by so much positivity, yet, the enemy wanted me to isolate myself, away from the love and nurturing required to bring my dry bones back to life. Seeing all those people worshiping and praising God's name and being a part of something bigger than my eyes could see, I was being restored and guided to the path that was truly intended for me.

"I remember the night I first met you." Marcel laughed as he began to reminisce on the day, he saw me in the hotel lobby, a weekend I wanted to forget.

"You walked in the room like you owned it, with such radiance and confidence. I wanted to get to know who that woman was. But listening to your story over these last few days, I would have never imagined, just looking at you, that you experienced so much trauma in your life. Corrie, you are the true definition of a fighter."

Fighting back tears, I tried to smile but all I could think about was the pain I felt when I found out my father passed away. The transgressions of my life made me into such a cry baby. I didn't want to imagine how disappointed he may have been with me and how I had let him down for the last time by not showing up when I was needed the most. Reaching for my hand, Marcel looked me directly in the eyes. "Whatever you're thinking, it's not your fault and it wasn't meant for you to carry that pain the way you have." Leaning over, he kissed me on the forehead and reached for a napkin to wipe away the tears that began to roll down my face. "We're going to get through this together and everything will be alright. You must have faith and believe it. I got you girl!" We both laughed at his last comment because we knew how corny he sounded saying it. But I believed him, and I was thankful that God placed him in my life. It was right on time.

Chapter 25

Let us draw near with a true heart in full assurance of faith, having our hearts sprinkled from an evil conscience, and our bodies washed with pure water. Let us hold fast the profession of our faith without wavering; (for He is faithful that promised;)

Hebrews 10:22-23 KJV

How many times have we taken life into our own hands, thinking we were in control and the keepers of our own destiny? Or better yet, how many times have we said we were going to trust God, just to doubt His capabilities all because things weren't happening according to our own timing? For me, I can raise my hand to both questions, knowing many times in my life I leaned into my own understanding. The money was not coming fast enough so I went out to get it a much faster way, or, I didn't want to deal with being lonely, so I settled for whomever would give me the attention I thought I needed. It is hard to accept the beauty of life when the trials become harder for us to bear and we expect life to be perfect. We compare our lives to others, not seeing the trials they also face when no one is looking. Or, we're able to bury the pain so deeply that you could not see that I was suicidal, or battling a drug addiction, or alcoholism. All I displayed was my fancy cars and my luxurious, empty house that everyone wanted. Yet, if you really walked in my shoes, you would give my life back at the snap of a finger. If you endured my pain, my loss, my depression, you would have been able to see that I am no different from anyone else walking through this dark valley.

God never intended for life on earth to be simple. He never said we wouldn't constantly be tested, learning to take up our cross and carry it as Jesus did for us. We are being sculpted, learning to endure as we run the race set in front of us, preparing us for the kingdom of heaven. Yet, I got caught up in the worldly things, eager to make my life look like those on the television. I wanted to show people that I could be better than my mother, constantly having to prove myself to others when the only standards I was required to live up to, were the one's God expected me to. I was being humbled by Him and it did not feel good. Yet, He was placing Godly people in my life to help me, to encourage me, and to push me beyond my expectations. Tasha encouraged me to open my mind and my soul to God's word, the bible. Marcel took it one extra step and drove me to the church, for fellowship and to open my heart to other likeminded individuals. I didn't realize what I needed until it was right in front of me. I wasn't fixated on how we met, but only the role they played in getting my life back on track.

I recall on numerous occasions, telling Tasha, not this Sunday but the next. Or completely ignoring her calls on Sunday morning all together. I made excuses and found other things to occupy my time, never considering tomorrow is not promised to any of us. God never stamped us with an expiration date and said you have X amount of time to get your life together. No one knows the time nor the hour but Him. Those who woke up this morning were blessed and those who did not, went to bed with the expectancy of seeing another day. So easily we are caught up in all the expectations we have placed on life, we fail to realize it is not ours to dictate.

As I began telling you my life story, it stated, I was not born into a life of riches, misunderstood, with little guidance, I lived recklessly with no cares of the consequences. Going from immature to sinful, I resisted correction, blatantly ignoring the path that was set before me. I wanted to go my own route and order my own steps. In the end, I was placed in reverse and forced to start over, but not without suffering the consequences of all my actions. And I do mean all! No matter how much you want to believe it, things will get worse before they start to get better. But if you trust in Him and keep the faith, the process won't hurt as bad. The bible says,

Now the works of the flesh are manifest, which are these, adultery, fornication, uncleanness, lasciviousness, idolatry, witchcraft, hatred, variance, emulations, wrath, strife, seditions, heresies, envying's, murders, drunkenness, revellings, and such like: of the which I tell you before, as I have also told you in time past, that they which do such things shall not inherit the kingdom of God.

Galatians 5:19-21 KJV

I experienced every single one of these sinful natures. My life consisted of everything these verses say, and I openly admit I am a sinner in need of saving. I can't see myself living eternity in a world worse than what we are living in now. I can't endure the sufferings greater than what I have already endured. I am tired and tired of running. My mother committed suicide, my brother was killed unexpectedly, both during my adolescent years. For most of my life, all I have known is sexual immorality, not respecting my body, which is a temple where the Holy Spirit dwell. I rejected discipline, not wanting anyone to tell me the things I consistently engaged in regularly was sinful and harmful to myself and others around me. And if you heard my mouth, you would think I should walk around with it covered up with duct tape. I woke up from parties, not able to remember what happened the night before due to being highly intoxicated.

You see, when we know better, we do better. And some of us, even now, will know better but not care because we only want what our hearts desire and don't comprehend the consequences that truly lie ahead. For those people, I pray for. My heart aches for them and I want so badly for them to have the opportunity to enter the Kingdom of Heaven. I'm not perfect, and even now as I tell you my story, I have still unknowingly sinned today because I was born into sin and continue to make foolish decisions. However, the difference between now and then, I recognize my flaws and I stand to have them corrected so that I will never do them again. My flesh is weak, and I am constantly tempted by the desires of my own heart, selfishly wanting to fill that urge, one foot towards heaven and the other buried in this world. But it is at those times that I am redirected and reminded of how detrimental it would be to my life. That, my friends, is wisdom and the knowledge of knowing right from wrong, inspired by the Holy Spirit.

As I continued to fight through my everyday temptations, wanting my old life back but knowing I needed to walk into my purpose, I struggled with acceptance. What if I never find a job making the money I was making in the clubs and at the spa?

What if I lose my house because I can no longer pay my bills? What will I say when people ask me about my previous employment? So many questions and I wanted immediate answers. It felt like I was asking God for my life's itinerary before I was willing to give it all up. Afraid of failure, the enemy was implanted in my mind deeply. And as I continued my journey, I became stronger and more accepting of the transition I was about to face.

Chapter 26

Screaming with excitement from the top of his lungs, Marcel was in the front room yelling like Saints fans the year New Orleans won the Super Bowl. I was laying peacefully in my bed and he stayed on the sofa. Grabbing my robe to see what all the commotion was about; I quickly made my way into the living area. He was standing there with his cell phone in his hand and a huge grin on his face.

"I have some really great news!"

"O.K, so let's hear it."

"Actually, I have more than just one thing to tell you." Overwhelmed with excitement, he did not know which news to give me first.

"First of all, let me tell you good morning. You look just as beautiful as I remembered from the morning waking up to you in the hotel room in New York. Secondly…. The broker just called; your building sold for over half of a million dollars. Apparently, you were sitting on a goldmine and that was the best investment you could have ever made."

Holding my composure, I was speechless. I didn't want to set myself up for disappointment, considering we still had to complete closing before everything could be finalized but I could feel the blessings in the air. "So, what is the other thing?" Anxious to hear something more about my case, rather than the fact I was completely unemployed, considering there was no club for me to go back to and no building left for me to prostitute out of. But I convinced myself it was for the better and a new beginning to a better me.

"O.K, so, the other thing I wanted to tell you, the private investigators have located the whereabouts of Nicholas."

"That's great! This means he can clear my name."

"Not exactly Co. He's dead."

"What? How is this good news? What happened?" My heart dropped. Although I was highly disgusted that he would leave me high and dry to take the wrap for something I did not do, I still loved him. I still cared for him. And he was still the only one who looked out for me when I needed him the most. Attempting not to show the true pain I was feeling inside, I got up and walked into my room. I needed a moment to register everything Marcel just told me, and I needed to grieve.

Laying in my bed listening to Nick's voicemails over and over, I could not stop the pain and I cried so hard, I knew Marcel could hear me, but I did not care. I wanted him to tell me he was lying and that he was somewhere in protective custody until the hearing. I was ready to face him in court and testify against him to fight for my innocence. But never in a million years was I prepared to say goodbye forever.

One hour went by before there was a knock at the door. I knew it was Marcel, but I did not have the energy to face him. I did not want him to know how deeply in love I was and how his news devastated my soul. What he thought would be good for my case, set me back an entire decade. So much death consumed my entire life and all my loved ones were leaving me prematurely. My heart could not fathom the pain and I wanted it to stop beating so I could no longer hurt anymore.

Opening the door, Marcel tip toed towards me. "Co is it ok if I come in?" Already near the bed, there was no point in me telling him no. "I'm really sorry for your loss and I'm hear if you want to talk about it. I didn't mean to sound excited about his death. I was just thinking how great this was for your case and makes it much easier to get it thrown out of court."

"It's not your fault. Can you hold me?"

Desperately in need of consoling, I did not realize what my mouth was saying, and I did not care. I just wanted to be in someone's arms and Marcel was that perfect person. He took off his shoes before climbing in the bed beside me and placing his arm gently around my waist. We laid silently in the dark as I continued to cry. My life seemed to be full of tears with less understanding in each situation.

"Did they say how he died? Did he suffer?"

"Corrie, I don't think we should go into details on how he…"

"Please. I need to know." Cutting him off, I wanted every detail of what he knew.

"His body was found washed ashore on the beach. They are thinking it was drug related because he was tortured. All fingers and toes were missing, and he barely had any teeth left in his mouth. There were gunshot wombs in several areas of his body."

With every gruesome thought, I whaled louder and harder to the visual. How can someone do something so terrible to a person with no remorse? And his wife, I knew she was hurting much more considering all he had put her through. She went from going through a divorce to becoming a widow. Unable to reach out, all I could do was close my eyes and pray. I knew Nick wasn't a good person, but he had a good heart. I prayed that God would have mercy on his soul so that one day I could see him again. I prayed for forgiveness for all the things I created in their marriage, the pain, the separation, and the grief. And as badly as I wanted to pay my last respects at the funeral, I knew I could never show my face. I could not say my goodbyes or be in the presence of his family without getting the dirty looks and the whispers of disgust. That chapter of my life closed with Nick's death and it was time for me to push forward, start over, and never look back.

Marcel was at my side every day, fixing me breakfast, lunch and dinner. He cleaned, did laundry, and even took care of all the paperwork for the selling of the property. And even on Sunday's when I did not want to do anything, he brought me his laptop and sat with me as we watched church online. For an entire month he selflessly placed my needs before his own, going from a business relationship to truly being one of my best friends. He knew the deepest of my secrets and was willing to withstand the emotional rollercoasters I would often go through. My instability created a reason for him to stand strong and fight even when I wanted to give up. The only time I left the house was when it was time to show my face in court. And hearing Nick's name was very hard for me, holding back tears, knowing he never deserved anything that happened to him.

"Ms. Matthews, I extend deep sympathy to you during this moment and I hope that you are able to put this all behind you and start a new life. In conclusion, you are free to go home. It won't be necessary for you to serve any more time for you have been through enough."

Hearing the word free coming out of the judge's mouth brought great joy and sorrow, both at the same time. It was not how I expected everything to end. In less than a year, my life shifted an entire three-sixty. First the club and Deslyn, who moved back to her country once her house sold, followed by the final closing of the spa. I knew the time would come for Nick to give up his wicked ways of hustling and if I would have told him, he may have listened to me. Yet, I was too caught up on my wants and needs to consider the dangerous game he was playing. Now all I could do is pick up the pieces and start over with what was left.

BOOK THREE

THE DELIVERANCE OF CORRIE MATTHEWS

Chapter 27

Thinking back over my life, I wasn't half the woman I am today. Just like the saying goes, although I am not where I want to be, I was not where I used to be. As soon as my court case was over, I knew I needed to be in church, thanking God for my freedom. I could have been in prison, or even worse, I could be dead, but he kept me. Knee deep in my wicked ways, I was ready to turn away from my past and walk into my future.

Sunday morning, I was up and dressed, waiting for Tasha to arrive. I called her the night before to make sure it was ok for us to ride to church together. Marcel finally returned to Atlanta, and I was slowly picking up the pieces for a brand-new day. I would be lying if I said Nick did not cross my mind often. With all the loss I experienced, I knew that pain well, but refused to allow it to consume me. I grieved. I was angry and often lonely, but I slowly began to let go.

As we arrived in the shopping center parking lot, I noticed lots more people attending than the night Marcel and I were there for prayer and worship. "You ready ma'am?", Tasha asked with determination in her voice. As many times she asked me to attend church with her, the day finally arrived when I was ready. Dressed in my Sunday's best, I could not help but notice the many who were casual, jeans and a dress top. But I was unbothered, walking inside with my head held high and Tasha right by my side, I once again needed to be the center of attention, even outside of my usual environment. Although, Jessica was the only familiar face I recognized and who knew of me, she would not be the only once we were done with all the meet and greets. I was approached by many friendly faces, from the pastor's wife all the way down to regulars who served, amazed by the many who volunteered their time to assist others. And when the music rung out into the common areas, I knew, like the last time, it was time to move towards the sanctuary for worship.

There was no better feeling than the one from being among people who did not judge me and who welcomed me with no stipulations. Hiding my past transgressions and pain inside, I sung along to the words on the big screen centered on stage, as an overflow of emotions consumed me. Before I knew it, I was crying. Unable to control it, I just kept singing along, "Oh the overwhelming, never ending, reckless love of God". The words were healing and spoke right to my soul, feeling every verse as it pertained to my life. No matter how hard I ran from Him, he chased me down and continued to fight for me, letting me know I was His. Tasha tried to hand me some Kleenex, but I refused, allowing the release of my fears with every tear that trickled down my face. But if that was not enough, the message was even deeper than the songs we worshiped to. It was as if he was preaching directly to me, on a soul that was weary. In the message, he told us to endure to the end and to stay in the presence of God, seeking Him daily in the word and never ceasing. And as he closed, he prayed for healing over all our lives. Not completely where I wanted to be, I knew it was a start from where I used to be. I could feel a shift in my thought process as I became eager to learn more and to grow.

Walking over to the campus bookstore to grab a free C.D of the service once we let out, I noticed a brochure of small groups with dates and times listed. I picked one up and placed it in my purse, making it a point to look over once I got home. I knew being around positivity would allow me the healing I needed and was good for my premature, spiritual development.

"Corrie, want to go grab a bite to eat?" Tasha asked as she was ending a conversation with one of the prayer team members. "This is Kevin. He and his wife led the small group that I was in a few months back."

"Hello." Kevin reached out to shake my hand. But my body froze, and I could not return the gesture to shake his, staring at his noticeable face as one of my clients from the spa. It was only months since our last encounter and now, there I was, starring a part of my past right in the face.

"Corrie is everything O.K.?", Tasha asked, not comprehending why I was not responding to Kevin's greeting. I knew he must have recognized me as well.

"It's O.K Corrie. Very nice to have you join us. Hope to see you around more often.", Kevin smiled and walked off to join his family as my body still refused to move. I watched as he returned to his wife and kids, wondering if she had any idea what type of person she was married to. What sort of lie was he telling her to explain the whips I remember putting on his back week after week? Not only that, but who was he seeing now that I was out of the picture?

"I don't know what just happened but let's get you out of here.", Tasha turned my body towards the door and led me out as I walked to the car in disbelief. Understanding everyone has a past, some darker than others, I was not judging Kevin. I just did not think my past would follow me into church, and during a time I was seeking a fresh start. No matter our sins and choices of living, we all have the option to turn our lives around and make better decisions.

As we approached the car, Tasha was full of so many questions, but I was clueless on how to answer any of them. I no longer indulged in a life of promiscuity and I did not desire to talk about it. Other than the club, she knew nothing about my secrets and the spa. So rather than stirring up a conversation, I remained quiet, wondering if I could ever step foot inside that church building again without feeling condemned. And I knew I could not tell anyone the truth about Kevin. Not only would Tasha not believe me, she would most likely judge me and think I was making excuses to not attend church. And who was I to publicly embarrass another family and be the reason for them to seek another church? Rather than continuing to dwell on it, I tried to focus on more positive things and not allow for the enemy to ruin my day.

"You want to grab a bite to eat?" Seeing I would not entertain the conversation she was attempting to stir up, she changed the subject. But my appetite was nonexistent and all I wanted to do was go home and get ready for the week ahead. Vanessa was scheduled to return from camp the following Friday, which only gave me barely two weeks, with lots of preparation ahead. Not to mention, I still needed to find a job before my savings account depleted.

"No, I'm really not that hungry. And I have some stuff around the house I need to work on."

"If you say so." Not wanting to put up a fight, Tasha drove me home as expected and stayed in her car as I got out and we said our goodbyes. "Let me know if you need anything or want to talk. I'm here for you Co."

"Thanks girl." I waved goodbye once again and walked to the front door, keys in hand, waiting for her to pull off. But when she was out of sight, I turned around, got into my car, and drove to the other side of town, where the old shop was located. Wanting to lay eyes on it one more time, I needed to know I was really done with my past and ready to move completely forward on my own without being forced by someone else.

Taking my seeing Kevin as some sort of sign, I needed closure. Did I really expect to be able to walk into the church and everything be washed away just like that? I still felt pain from Nick's death, wanting to believe the spa was the only thing I had left to remember him and the only familiar place I felt needed. It was my safety net. It was the first thing I built on my own, with the investment of Nick. I sat in the parking lot, crying like a baby, wishing all the pain would go away. Praying for a brighter tomorrow but just trying to understand how to get through the day, it was hard for me to grasp how all the trusting in God was really going to help me. When was He going to break the chains that held me in bondage for so many years? How long would it take for the pain to fade and for me to no longer feel uncomfortable? With all the devastation I experienced for so long, surely, He would hear my cry out to Him now and come take it all away, reconstruct my entire life and make me a better person overnight. But it did not work like that and He was still in control.

Chapter 28

Staying faithful and spending as much time as possible into the word, I searched for a clearer understanding of this thing called life. I wanted to become stronger, bolder, wiser, and confident in the person whom I was becoming. Yet, I was spiritually empty, yearning for someone or something to pour into me and guide me in the right direction so I did not backslide into my old habits.

It was only Monday and everything I absorbed from church the day before had already gone out of the window. I lacked focus and could only concentrate on the devastations in my life. I was reading the book of Genesis all over again, but my attention would soon deviate from the bible and on the what ifs. What could I have done differently to be on a better path? Or maybe this was all in God's plan. Thinking to myself how it took over twenty years for Joseph to reach his purpose and all the suffering he endured, I did not have twenty more years to wait. I spent years wandering in the wilderness and now I was ready to clean my life up and give everything to God. But from my understanding, I wanted to be free instantly, to be removed from the pit and washed clean from all past transgressions. Feeling defeated, I yelled out loud, "help me God!", not knowing what else to do. I was forced to be still, left to sit there and wait it out until the next segment of God's divine plan, yet I was not alone. It was uncomfortable, and I was convinced the enemy gotten the best of me, whispering in my ear, I was a terrible person and there was no way God was listening after the mess I made so many times.

Attempting to regroup and refocus my thought process on something more positive, I needed to stop allowing negativity to play on my inner peace. The enemy comes to steal, kill, and destroy and for whatever reason, I was constantly on his list. Positive Corrie, think positive. I grabbed my purse and searched for the small group paper I picked up from the church the day before. Looking over the list at all the different options, I decided to reach out to one. So many to choose from, I needed to be around women who could relate to me, one for single women in my age group. Reaching for my phone, I called the number listed on the paper.

"Hello." A friendly voice answered on the second ring.

"Hi, is this Amber?"

"Yes, it is. How can I help you?"

"My name is Corrie and I was wanting to join your small group."

"Yes, of course! I'm so glad you reached out. I would love for you to be a part of my group. Right now, we have five other women attending. I can give you my address. We meet at my apartment every Wednesday night at seven." Not the average person I would normally seek to hang out with, I was unsure of what I was getting myself into. I needed good, Godly women in my life which meant I needed to become more open minded and welcoming.

"Can you text me your address? I'm sure seven will be just fine."

"Sure thing. I will text it to you as soon as we hang up and I look forward to meeting you."

"Thanks" We hung up the phone and within ten seconds I was receiving a text of her address. Hoping there was no one in this group who I would recognize and who would recognize me, I was seeking unfamiliar faces to connect with. It was time for me to be more transparent with others and allow someone in, understanding it was not healthy for me to go through life alone. And especially since I was going to need emotional support with being a parent and learning how to raise a teenager. Only eleven days until Vanessa arrived from camp, I failed already by not making contact. I wanted to make sure I was prepared before our first conversation, making myself emotionally available to her and not for her to see how dysfunctional her mother truly was. There were still some things I needed to deal with before the big day.

After hanging up, I decided to make myself a snack and indulge in some television for an hour or so. Still focused on the small group and what may have been expected of me, I knew speaking about my life would be a part of the healing process. But how open would I have to be? I knew I was not the only one who experienced hardships, death, and disappointments. But I'm sure I would be the only ex stripper slash prostitute to ever step foot in their presence. Honestly speaking, my lifestyle was something most would watch on a Lifetime channel, but never experienced in real life. Attempting not to overthink things and talk myself out of going, I flipped through the channels to allow myself to focus on something else. Until Wednesday was to come, I could only live for Monday, seeking my purpose in all it had in store for me.

Chapter 29

Have you ever felt like God wasn't listening? Like His presence was no longer near and you were left all alone to figure life out on your own? It's like in the book of Psalms when King David cried out to God, and I was feeling like David.

Hear me when I call, O God of my righteousness: thou hast enlarged me when I was in distress: have mercy upon me and hear my prayer.

Psalms 4:1 KJV

It was as if, trying to make things right and staying on a straight path was becoming harder to bear. The not knowing and expectations that I could no longer control was eating me up inside. There was no steady income coming in and I had no idea when I would get a job. And then there was the wondering of if the job would be to my likings, what kind of schedule would I be on and how would it fit my everyday routine? My mind raced for hours and I wanted all of it to stop. I understood I could not look past the day into my tomorrows and that God was in control. However, my thoughts over my life were nothing more than what anyone else would have expected for theirs. How can you not wonder about tomorrow when lies of the enemy are starring you directly in the face? Every day I felt free from the club and the spa, was another day of being enslaved by doubt and all the possibilities. I knew I could not take any more failures to come.

Wednesday showed up faster than I expected. That morning was spent majority of the time online, filling out job applications, although I really did not have much professional job experience. I was too embarrassed to list the club as my most recent job. The only leverage I had was putting my experience as running a business as a spa owner. I applied for lots of listings for massage therapists, in hopes of someone calling me back soon. Knowing Vanessa was on the way, I expected to obtain something before she arrived, so I would not have to explain what I'd been doing beforehand. Being a responsible adult on a straight path was becoming stressful and depressing. Annoyed by all the questions on the job applications, I slammed my laptop shut and closed my eyes for a moment. But in that time, I began to feel overwhelmingly emotional. Only a few weeks in, I was ready to give up on everything, no longer feeling this life was meant for me. The process of obtaining a job was stressful and the waiting was emotionally draining. Not to mention, the pay sucked. There was no way I could afford anything I have now on the salary these positions were offering. Welcome to the real world, I thought to myself. My life ruined since birth and now I was suffering the consequences of my bad decisions, feeling I was never destined for anything other than a hard knock life.

Grabbing my car keys and my purse, I drove to an adult entertainment club I knew of on the other side of town, no longer considering what Vanessa would think if she knew her mother was a dancer, I no longer cared. All I wanted was my old life back of feeling wanted and accepted. I wanted to be in a position of importance and make good money while doing it.

As I pulled up, I noticed much younger, more in shape girls walking inside. Sitting in the parking lot observing the environment, it took less than an hour before I began to feel out of place and something inside of me was telling me to leave. As much as I craved taking the easy road, I realized there was no such thing and this life was no longer for me. I thought about Deslyn, and then Nick. One was deported back to her home and the other was no longer alive. It was God's grace that saved me and His mercy which allowed for me to start over on the right path. This life was never intended to last beyond the amount of time it did, and a new chapter was necessary. Starting the car, I pulled out of the parking lot and drove back to my house to revisit job applications. The enemy was attacking me from every angle, and I continued to give him power over my thoughts, but I was no longer interested in believing the lies he was telling me. Not understanding what God's plans were for me, I knew I needed to remain faithful and have patience. I knew there would not be days without pain and confusion. But given all I had already been through, what could be worse? I could not go back to what God already delivered me from.

As I drove, I prayed in silence. No radio, just me and God. What seemed like a broken prayer was my cry out for help. I needed to feel His presence. "Dear God, give me strength where I am weak, and forgive me for all of my doubts. Help me to stay focused on You and not lean into my own understanding but trust Your will for my life. Amen."

I arrived at Amber's promptly at seven, not a minute early nor a minute later. Hesitantly I knocked at the door, wondering if I should have brought anything. A short, red head, answered with a bright smile. She had very distinct freckles and beautiful, green eyes, sort of like a cat. The other ladies were already there, everyone sitting around the television making small talk. "You must be Corrie." Everyone turned their attention towards me to get a peek at the new girl.

"That's me", trying to keep a welcoming smile on my face as though I did not already feel out of place.

"Come on in." She pointed at each of the other ladies as she told me their names. There was Tracie, Courtney, Elizabeth, Shannon, and Lisa, all extending a friendly smile as they waved. I walked over and sat on one of the bright orange lawn chairs she set up in the living area.

"So, this is actually only our second week meeting, so you haven't really missed anything." I just smiled, not much of a social butterfly in the beginning, I was at a loss for words but was attempting to not seem uptight in a room full of so many bubbly personalities. My attention was directly on Amber as she spoke, avoiding eye contact with the others. As she suggested everyone to reintroduce themselves, so I could become familiar with the group, the only thing I was focused on was how truthful should I be, not interested in indulging too much information during the first meeting. I was always one to overthink things rather than relaxing.

Amber went first since she was the leader. From what I gathered, she was a single mother of two, and only been attending the church for a little over a year. Not too much older than I, she worked as a paralegal at a nearby law firm. As she spoke, she constantly played with the curls of her red hair and could never stop smiling. Next was Shannon, who seemed to be the oldest of the group. She was divorced with no kids and sold insurance for a living. Although she did not smile as much as Amber, she still displayed a peaceful demeanor. Tracie was the one in the group who seemed to have no worries in the world. She worked as a surgical technician and spoke very highly of her parents and upbringing, still living in the same house. She sat in the corner, Indian style, still wearing her scrubs, obviously coming straight to the meeting from work. Courtney was a college student, working on her pharmacy residency. She sat on the sofa, stuffing her mouth with snacks and talking with her mouth full. Being at the church the longest, she was very involved in lots of different ministries.

When it got around to Elizabeth and Lisa, both were hesitant to speak, a lot like myself. They looked at each other to see who would go first. Rather than waiting, I decided to speak up and introduce myself while I still had the nerve to do so. Glad to see I was not the only one in the room who was not eager to share information on self, I felt I could relate to them more than I could to the others.

"As you all know, my name is Corrie. I have only been attending the church for a few weeks and I am currently transitioning from being a business owner to seeking full time employment."

"Oh! What is it that you do?", Courtney asked with a mouth full of food.

"I am a licensed massage therapist." I said believingly, liking how it sounded once I said it out loud.

"My mother is actually the vice-president over at the technical institute in downtown Tampa and I heard her telling someone the massage therapy instructor quit." Elizabeth, snapping out of her bashful demeanor, became indulged in the conversation and I was even more intrigued by the idea of a job doing what I love. "Do you have any teaching experience?"

"No, I've never been an instructor, but I have several years of experience."

"I'll ask her about it when I get home. Give me your number so I can text you."

Exchanging numbers, I became hopeful and full of joy. Thinking to myself, I was so glad I decided to come to the group. It wasn't as bad as I expected, and I possibly landed a job doing something I could be good at. I also found out that Elizabeth, Liz as I began to call her over time because she reminded me so much of the bartender from the club, was an ex-stripper like myself. Although I never volunteered that information, she became more of an open book once I started talking first. She lived a very rebellious, reckless life for years until someone invited her to a small group, which led her to attending services at the church and giving her life to God.

Lastly, there was Lisa. When it came time for her to speak, I found out she was a recovering alcoholic two months pregnant, and even though this was a singles group, she had a boyfriend with whom she was cohabitating with. I understood why she was last in the introductions, relating to the feelings of shame and guilt, being judged even more. Yet, I continued to keep my guard up for the time being.

Gathering among such a diverse group of women brought comfort and helped me to relax more as we talked and engaged in conversation wrapped around everyday life. For two hours, I was no longer that anti-social, loner I tried so hard to remain, welcoming friendship and learning how I could relate to so many of the things these other women were talking about. Once we come to the realization of everyone going through something, it makes life much easier to exist in, understanding we all are fighting some sort of battle. Just like Jesus, we all carry our own cross and suffer in one way or another. Just because some are better at hiding the pain does not mean it is not there. Which explains drug addiction, alcoholism, and self-inflicted pain. My copping mechanism was the fake love I was receiving from so many unfamiliar men just to fill the void of emptiness which remained constant throughout my life because I did not know how to fight back. I did not realize the battle I was facing, in which we all are facing, is in a different realm from what our eyes could see, and only God can get us through it if we call on Him and trust in His every word. Slowly, I was learning how to fight back.

Before parting ways, Amber led us in prayer. Everyone hugged, and we said our goodbyes until our next meeting a week later.

Chapter 30

Every day of my new journey was a test… is a test. I struggled to understand my purpose and to hear God's voice, not knowing what it was I was listening for. It felt like I was playing chess with life, attempting to avoid the enemy and preventing him from stealing my crown. I was a newborn in my Christian faith, still learning how to crawl and all the amazing things He equipped me with. Yet, struggling with my emotions was the one thing I could not fathom. One day I would be fine and the next, I would feel pain, disappointment, and loneliness. It was in those days that I prayed more, I worshipped more, and I cried out to Him, no longer expecting my feelings to just disappear, but reassuring myself He was there, standing in the midst of my struggles and there to push me through it with His strength.

On Thursday, the day after my first small group meeting, I met with Tasha for lunch to share my experience and tell her all about the other ladies. It was like having a new toy that I could not stop talking about and I could not wait until the following week, so I could enjoy it once more. But as I spoke, I could not help but notice a look of emptiness on Tasha's face. Something was bothering her, and she was keeping silent. Caught up in the things of my life, I failed to keep up with the one whom was pouring into it and pushing me through along the way. It was through her I realized the true meaning of friendship, fellowship, and sisterhood. She stood by me through the worse and encouraged me when I wanted to give up on myself. It was in those days I finally realized what she meant when she said she was sent to me, not physically, but spiritually. She was drawn to me with compassion and a desire to love on me when I could not love myself.

"Tasha, what's wrong?" Through her usual smile she just looked at me and replied with, "nothing". But I could see past the disguise she was trying to hide behind. She was bothered and had a feeling of unease. I could sense it because I too suffered from this kind of pain and displayed the same look on many occasions. But since she wanted to remain silent, I felt compelled to do what I never done before in life. Sliding my chair close to hers, I reached for her hand and began to pray, allowing the Holy Spirit to lead me because I did not know what to say.

"Dear Heavenly Father, I just want to start by thanking You for Your unconditional love, for Your mercy, and for Your strength. Father I pray over the life of Tasha, that whatever it is she is going through, You comfort her and strengthen her to push through, with the assurance that You go before her, preparing her for whatever it is You have called her to do for the glory of your kingdom. If it is healing, Father I pray for You to heal her in only the way You can and only if it is in Your will. Father I pray for You to help us to not lean into our own understanding, but to seek You first in every situation and circumstance. In Jesus' name. Amen."

When I opened my eyes, Tasha's face was wet, and her eyes were full of tears. She cried in silence and her pain overshadowed her joy. As I reached out to wrap my arms around her frail body for comfort, I wanted to be there through everything she was going through, but not wanting to push her to talk until she was ready. At that moment, from the outside looking in, all I could see was the devastation my closest friend was experiencing. Something was eating away at her soul, bringing her down into depression, and attempting to draw her away from God's promise. From the outside, I was focused on the potential outcomes of Tasha's pain once all was said and done, and this passed.

Tasha's faith was solid. She stood firm in God's word and was a motivator, inspirator, and encourager to those who were weak in their beliefs. We all need someone who will walk with us from our potential to our purpose and nothing happens by coincidence. God puts people in our lives for a reason and to draw us closer to our destiny. Whether only for a season or a lifetime, it is never an accident. So, from the outside looking in, all I could see was the enemy's attempt to do harm to Tasha's spiritual growth, to make her weak, and prevent her from doing the work of God she was called to do.

Satan wants our identity and demise and will stop at nothing until he succeeds, and I knew Tasha's strength would prevail because she remained unmoved, knowing that the power of God was stronger than any obstacle she could ever endure. Little did I know, this attack was not on her, but created as a part of my battle. Little did I know, it was God's plan to push me closer to my divine purpose, using her throughout the process to make me stronger and to open my eyes to a much bigger picture. Little did I know, she was my mentor and I would one day pick up where she left off, inspiring others to press forward and keep their eyes fixed on Jesus. It was on that day, Thursday, August twenty-seventh, I realized the enemy would stop at nothing to destroy me, but God had my best interest at heart and would get all glory and praise when it was all said and done. Tasha's battle was not her battle. It was part of mine. So, when she spoke those four words, "Corrie, I have cancer", I knew it was another test of my faith and pain began to creep in once more.

Chapter 31

Friday morning was hard. Meditating on Tasha's words all night, I prayed for her healing every time I thought about it. I was not ready for my friend to leave me, overthinking the situation as though I already knew the outcome. She refused chemo, said she did not want to be any sicker than she already was and how she wanted whatever God desired for her life. Afterall, He alone, is the author and finisher of everything. I admired her faith. No matter the situation, she remained hopeful. I reminisced on the day we first met, how she was so determined to force her way into my life and create a friendship I did not imagine being a part of. All I could do was smile, believing every encounter is for a reason.

Around a quarter to ten, my phone began to buzz, still being on vibrate from the night before so I could not be disturbed. It was Liz from my small group. I picked up immediately in anticipation of hearing some good news about the instructor position she was telling me about. But instead, she was calling to see if I would be interested in attending a Women's Conference with her on Saturday. "Sure thing", I replied, hoping this would be my opportunity to make a good impression and pick her brain about interviewing with her mom. And, it would give me some individual bonding time to get to know who she really was when she was not among the other ladies.

Not two minutes after ending the call, my phone began to buzz again. Thinking it was Liz calling back, I looked at the screen to notice it was Justin calling. Knowing eventually, I would have to have a conversation with him more sooner than later, I hesitantly picked up.

"Good morning", I answered. Finally, ready to make amends and put the past behind us. Regardless of my feelings for Justin, he stepped up in an area I did not and remained the constant parent in our daughter's life, and for that, I was grateful. I could never explain the condemnation I felt for not being there. Back then, I did not understand the feelings I was feeling as being such. It felt like guilt that pierced my heart and I tuned it out through my bad habits and poor decision making. Knowing eventually this day would come, I was ready to face my fears.

"What's up?", Justin asked, with his distinctive, New York accent. Seeming a little vague, I could tell he was feeling me out to see what kind of mood I was in.

"You tell me. Afterall, you're the one calling my phone first thing in the morning."

Justin laughed, knowing I was always known to be a smart mouth to hide what I was truly feeling. Deep inside I wanted to apologize for being an absent parent from our daughter's life for so long. Yet, I waited for him to begin the conversation on Vanessa, so we could finally clear the air. I needed him to let me in on her likes and dislikes, not wanting to admit that, once again, I failed to reach out because of all the issues I was dealing with.

 "Well Co, if you must know why I have chosen to bless your morning with my voice…" he paused, beginning to laugh sarcastically. "Honestly, with all joking aside, you crossed my mind. Not to mention, with Vanessa getting out of camp soon, I was thinking I could be down there to help you out with the transition and adjustment."

"Really?" I was blushing, and my heart was filled with so much joy and relief at the same time. I could feel God tearing down my walls with every situation I was up against and it was a good feeling. Contemplating night and day, I had no idea how this transition would come to pass, and I was standing on faith, God would see me through it. Even if she did not like me, I convinced myself that was normal, and she was just going through a teenage phase.

"So, you're actually O.K with that?" Justin was as surprised of my answer as I was in him mentioning the idea. I was happy we were able to get to a point where we could have a cordial conversation and co-parent, something my parents were never able to do.

"Yes, I am ecstatic of the idea and look forward to getting to know both, you and Vanessa." Still avoiding the reasoning to her sudden move, I did not want to spoil the conversation with my selfishness. I should have been there, and so many years were already lost.

"Vanessa will be fine. I did not know how you would accept this transition at first, considering you did not want her in the beginning. And now that she is older, I did not want to just bring her around to face rejection. But I'm glad everything worked out."

'You did not want her'…. I think those were the only words I heard coming from his mouth. Not the positive outcome of what he was saying, not how he was glad things were going to be better for her. But, the idea of me not wanting her. It was the second time I was hearing those words, the first coming from Nick. Recognizing the enemies attempt to break me once more, I immediately began to think of the positive outcome of the situation and how I was going to be a mother once more. And the glory of it all, I could no longer stay mad at myself for the things of my past because I buried them with all my other flaws.

Discovering God's grace gave me a second chance to make things right. Thanking God, I was no longer the girl from my past, I fought against the lies the enemy was telling me and allowed my joy to overshadow my doubts. I was going to be a good mother and I was ready to face whatever questions Vanessa had for me. I wanted faith beyond what Tasha was equipped with, being my inspiration to push through the obstacles and becoming even stronger than I was before.

Not realizing the silence, I heard Justin calling my name.

"Co, did you hang up?"

"No, I'm still here…. sorry."

"O.K, well, I have to go for now. It was good to connect and chop it up. I'll touch basis with you next week with my flight arrangements if that's cool with you."

"Yeah, definitely."

After saying our goodbyes and disconnecting the call, I laid in my bed wondering how Justin was really doing, how had life been treating him, and praying he too, would not tell me he was dying. With all the heaviness on my heart for Tasha, I was not prepared to face anymore tragedies. Although, I knew it would not be the end of disappointments and heartbreaks, the calm after the storm was nice for a change. I needed to regain my composure and focus on my continuous walk with God, rather than the transgressions that were continually being thrown my way. No longer wanting to play victim, I was slowly moving towards my destiny and gaining an understanding of who was in control this entire time. He has been walking with me and guiding me, but most importantly, protecting me from my life of destruction. Just the idea of Him never giving up on me, even when I refused to turn from my ways, made me feel loved and wanted by a Father who would never leave my side no matter how doubtful I may have become.

Chapter 32

We all could use a little bit more mercy, an outpour of grace. Our faith could be stronger, becoming more yielding to God's word; A little more understanding, loving, and forgiving of others. The point is, no matter our walk of life, none of us are perfect and we all were born in need of a savior. I never judge others because I know, knowing my story, I would not want them judging me. Not only that, but God is the final judge and we will all one day be held accountable for our actions, our unforgiveness, and our harsh judgements towards others.

On Saturday, I woke up early in attempt to do some cleaning before Liz arrived to pick me up for the event. Becoming more open to guests, I wanted my home more presentable to others. The expo started at ten and was scheduled to run throughout the day, with a lineup consisting of several motivational speakers and worship artists, with vendor booths and different food retailers as well. Unsure of what would be dress appropriate, I threw on a tan, wrap style romper and some platform sandals, accessorized with my gold hoop earrings and gold, long pendant necklace.

Liz arrived at my house promptly at noon, not wanting to arrive at the event soon as it started. Thinking she would want to come in to peek, instead, she stayed in the car and called my phone to let me know she was in the driveway waiting. Grabbing my keys and handbag, I locked up and jumped into the passenger side of her all black Jeep Wrangler. She was playing, MercyMe, Even If, blue toothed from her phone, and the words had me mesmerized as I stared at the screen on the dash, displaying the title and the artist.

"But God when you choose to leave mountains unmovable, give me the strength to be able to sing, it is well with my soul." Meditating on that verse, it was breathing life into every situation I faced. It gave me a deeper understanding of how the intent was not to break me, but to mold me into who I was destined to become. And although God has the power to remove every obstacle which makes us feel uncomfortable, He does not. I was moved by the song, taking out my phone to add it to my Pandora playlist. Through every song that played, I became more encouraged, as my list became even longer, giving me songs to turn to when I was home alone. Who knew that worship music was so comforting for the mind and spirit, allowing my thought process to become fixated on God's promise?

When we arrived at our destination, Liz and I walked at a slow pace to the front entrance, recapping our week and what was going on in our lives. Still not mentioning Vanessa and the fact I had a daughter, I brought up applying to jobs to see if she would mention anything else about the instructor position. But she didn't. Instead, she listened as I continued my ramble.

Receiving a handout from the greeter at the entrance, we flipped through to see which stage we would visit first. To my surprise, there was one speaker who stood out and caught my attention immediately…Tasha. She was hosting a segment on, 'Staying Faithful Throughout Life's Circumstances', and I was eager to hear what she had to say.

"This one seems interesting and it starts in less than ten minutes.", I pointed out to Liz, picking up the pace so I could hear everything from beginning to end. I did not wish to go into any details about knowing the speaker, nor how she was a member of our church, feeling it would open up a gateway to have to discuss how we met. I was not yet as transparent as I would like to have been, still afraid of being judged by her and the rest of the women in our group.

We took our seats right before Tasha appeared on stage, sitting directly on the front row so she would know I was there. She walked out so confidently, fearless and brave. Although I may have been the only one aware, you could not tell she was suffering from cancer and she did not let it stop her from doing God's work, remaining faithful to her calling. From my perception, I assumed Liz did not recognize who she was.

"Time is a nonrenewable resource… where is God in your time?" Beginning her speech with a question, the room went completely silent and everyone's attention was on Tasha, wondering what she would say next. I was searching for the answer in my mind, thinking about every calculated moment of my days. Did I put Him first or was it only about self?

"Seems like everything that could happen in life…all happened to me. Too embarrassed to tell my story, I didn't think many would listen, would secretly pass judgement, or whisper about it behind my back. But then I realized, it was not about what I wanted to do, but what God needed for me to share with others so that they too can find freedom and healing. I wanted to share how He delivered me and how every day, no matter the circumstance, I include Him in everything I do; reaching for

Christ even through my most difficult moments. It is our reactions, not the action itself, that determines the outcome."

Tasha paused for a moment, looking around the room to make sure she had everyone's attention before continuing. "For years, I was haunted by the idea of my father raping me every night when my mother would go to sleep, not knowing I was not even his biological child. I was adopted at a really young age. It didn't make it right, but it gave me an understanding to why he cared less. When I found out the truth, that my real parents were junkies and their only child, who was me, was taken by the state, I was already sixteen. All those years went by and I had been lied too, abused, broken down into nothing. I learned how to not fight, and to just give in to whatever others wanted of me. My dad did not love me, and my mother ignored what was staring her right in the face because she did not want to deal with it. But I was given a choice… a choice to be upset… a choice to rebel against the ones who raised me… or a choice to be grateful I was not stuck in the system. I chose silence."

My thoughts wondering from Tasha's speech to my upbringing, I fought to remain focused on what she was saying, not wanting to miss the message. Realizing she would never communicate to me in a one on one, the way she was at that moment, I was learning who she really was.

"I was sheltered, attending the best of private schools and having anything I wanted at my fingertips. Other than a little sexual abuse, my life appeared to others as perfect. Yet, I was hurting. I was fearful. And the only person I could tell on this earth who would believe a junkie's baby, was…nobody. To me, it sounded as if I were being ungrateful, believing my dad when he would say, if you tell, they'll take you away from us to live with strangers, creating a fear inside of me that would just grow through every incident. I began to seek comfort in middle school when, as an eighth-grade graduation gift, they gave us all bibles. After so many years of defeat, I began to read it, every morning and every night before I went to bed, failing to understand the true meaning because of it being the King James version. As a young teenager, I had no idea what my bible was saying to me but eager to learn. So, for Christmas, I asked my parents for a youth bible that I could actually read."

The crowd began to laugh, as I continued to relate to what Tasha was saying. Her sufferings were as messed up as mine, but she was able to establish the secret to remaining joyful, something I desperately needed.

"The more I indulged in my daily devotion, the more I began to pray, becoming intentional. And then I came across this verse, Psalms thirty-four, verse eight, that read, ***O taste and see that the Lord is good: blessed is the man that trusteth in Him.*** Putting those words to the test, I accepted the challenge. I began to talk to God about everything. He already knew my every thought, so I felt no condemnation by speaking them to Him boldly. Many of my prayers were answered and others were not. But never did I become discouraged because I knew, if He answered some, there was a reason for the ones that were not."

"My high school years were more peaceful than the previous years before, slowly learning how to put all of my trust and faith into my creator. But just as soon as you feel nothing can go wrong, that is when life's hurdles come tearing down your walls of peace. I can remember my first day of my freshman year of college. My parents dropped me off on campus, met with my new roommate, made sure I had everything I needed for the perfect semester, and they were killed in a tragic car accident driving back home. That was my first time ever feeling a loss like I felt, angry, disappointed, and heartbroken, leading up to a downhill spiral from there. Life was tough. It was during that time I learned my father possessed a gambling problem and my mother was struggling to maintain the bills during the last two years they were living. Their life insurance policy had lapsed, and I lost everything. The secrets were all being revealed, and their glamourous life turned out to be a phony because they were trying to keep up with a lifestyle they could not afford. Sure… they had burial policies, but nothing to leave behind to maintain the life I was accustomed to. I couldn't pay for that house or those cars they were making monthly payments on. I couldn't even afford groceries. Everything my parents worked so hard to obtain was lost. And when I thought things could not get any worse, two weeks after their funeral, I received notice I was being put out of school because my tuition check did not clear. There was no one for me to call to fix it and I didn't know what to do. I prayed day and night for God to help me, but my soul began to weaken as my prayers were seemingly being unanswered. And that is when my faith began to fail. I became weary, questioning why God would shift my life so profoundly and cause for my world to come caving in."

It was in Tasha's speech I realized how, when good things stop happening, that is when we need to hold firm to our faith the most. Embracing Tasha's pain as my own, I began to realize my transgressions were no larger than anyone else's. Although we go through different events, trials, battles, fears, and discomforts, we are all broken down in some sort of way. My thoughts began to go even deeper as I reflected of my readings of the bible and the life of Jesus. I could not imagine enduring the pain and suffering he endured for myself and others. Never once complaining, and yet, we tend to complain about the smallest amount of unease. As Tasha continued to speak, my comprehension of this thing called life began to shift and I was starting to view it through a completely different lens.

"I did what I had to do and got a job on campus and even applied for student loans, determined not to drop out of school. It was hard. I knew nothing about how cruel the world could be, and I was not prepared for all it would take me through. During my sophomore year, I fell in love, got pregnant, and was forced to drop out. I'm sure that was not the path my parents would have wanted me to take, but I was vulnerable and weak. I was walking through day to day life, empty and uncertain, no longer crying out to God for help. I stopped reading my bible, and the thought of going to church never crossed my mind. It's ironic how a change in life's events can cause you to turn away so easily but it was only proof that my faith wasn't as strong as I thought it would be. I convinced myself I had everything under control, and I was now the captain of my destiny. I moved off campus and into an apartment with my baby's daddy, thinking we would be a family. But instead, he became abusive… mentally, emotionally, and physically... beating me every time he would get angry. I was freshly in my twenties and all I wanted was love and to be wanted and appreciated. I believed the lies when he would tell me he was sorry. I believed him when he said he would never do it again, but he would. Crying myself to sleep became a regular trend for me and I adopted my new lifestyle as normal. I convinced myself that everyone goes through these kinds of situations, especially since I was sexually abused by my own father growing up. One day he beat me so badly, I lost our baby and ended up in the hospital for three days. Not only that, the doctor told me the damage was so severe... I would never be able to get pregnant again."

Tasha paused, fighting back tears, I knew those were the hardest words to come out of her mouth. I wanted to get up to console her so badly. Looking around the room at all the other many women attending, I could see the pain displayed on their faces as well. Even Liz was sitting next to me crying, as I reached for her hand to let her know everything would be ok.

"It was those events that made me rebel and forget everything I once believed in. I started smoking marijuana and became a stripper at a local club. No longer interested in the nickel and diming, minimum wage gigs, I needed fast money, so I could start my life over. The apartment I was living in belonged to my ex and with the lease only being in his name, I could not go back there. The police referred me to a shelter, which I lived in for months. I attended a community college by day and worked late nights, as many nights as I was allowed, staying busy to keep my mind off how broken my life became. Consumed in the right now's of life, I did not realize how dangerously I was really living. It was the evening, walking back to the shelter from a long night at the club, when a strange man came out of nowhere and held me at gunpoint."

Demonstrating to the audience, she held her left hand up to her head as if it were a gun, as she continued to speak into the microphone, yet still, never making eye contact. "He was aggressively holding me by my neck with his left hand and holding the gun, pointed directly to my face with his right. He took all my earnings from the night, which was about four hundred dollars, and I can remember closing my eyes and praying like I never prayed before since my parents were killed. Tears were pouring down my face. Asking God for mercy and protecting me from any harm, I didn't care about the money, but I wanted to keep my life. I knew God was not done with me and there was a reason behind the madness I was experiencing. I was placed in a season to make me cry out to Him. And I cried hard as I knew how that night. The guy ran off and I stood there, unharmed, weeping and praising God because I knew He was the one who kept me. Escaping death for a second time was my opportunity to choose God's way, which is why I stand here today, advocating for people to have faith and trust His plan for your lives despite the circumstances."

Finally realizing the truth to her story, I felt closer to Tasha and understood why she was so eager to pull me away from the club. It made sense to why she was so comfortable with being around so many broken women who were all experiencing something different in life, not afraid to speak truth into their situations. No matter how much I could not admit I needed her, I was glad she arrived when she did, ready to let her in on the things I kept bottled deep down inside and knowing it would make me feel much better to talk to someone who understood my pain. She was the one true person who I could trust, and I was thankful for her presence in my life.

Feeling encouraged, the crowd cheered and clapped, with a standing ovation, once Tasha was done. I was beyond proud of my friend and her accomplishments, for her bravery and boldness, being transparent with others and sharing her testimony. And although I was the only one in the crowd who knew her fight was not over, only God knew the outcome.

Chapter 33

__For our light affliction, which is but for a moment, worketh for us a far more exceeding and eternal weight of glory; While we look not at the things which are seen, but at the things which are not seen: for the things which are seen are temporal: but the things which are not seen are eternal.__

2 Corinthians 4:17-18 KJV

Later that night, I laid in the dark, sobbing my eyes out. Even after a perfect day out, it did not take long for my heart to become heavy, and the doubt to set in. I was thinking about Nick, which redirected my thoughts to Tasha and the idea of losing another close person in my life. Listening to her story and finally getting an idea of who she was and all she had been through, helped me to understand how she found peace with everything she was dealing with. But her story was not going to help me find mine. Although I was reading my bible, attending church, and now being a part of a small group, the pain did not instantly go away. I experienced my highs but very often there were lows, which continued to overpower my judgement. Nobody said there would never be troubles or heartaches just because we go through the motions. My battle was still ongoing, and I had yet to find a way to channel that energy into something positive. I became fearful of the future and once again, loneliness, fear, and worry were all beginning to control my thoughts. I picked up my phone to turn to my bible app for comfort, knowing the word would change my thought process and bring me back to peace. But once I opened it, I could not find the strength to read. I was grateful for all I was able to overcome yet saddened by the things I had not achieved.

The idea of us giving our lives to God and everything suddenly becoming perfect is so overrated and far from the truth. Becoming saved created more challenges, as I was always under attack. My strength and faith were constantly being tested and I continued to stumble. The pressure did not let up and I felt like I was going under, fighting to keep my head above the waves. If we live on this earth, we are constantly faced with more and more obstacles that will attempt to bring us down and drive us away from our faith. But the beauty of it all, no matter how many times we fall, it is by God's grace that we can get back up. It is our trust in Him that gives us the desire to do what is right, knowing He is in control and want nothing but good things for our lives. Yes, He delivered me from dancing and having sex for money, but I still worried about obtaining a job and being able to maintain. Knowing I could be in a grave right now or behind bars, I was thankful for everything God did for me, growing my faith and believing there was still another blessing left. I prayed for His comfort and I prayed for Him to heal my heart. Yet, I felt nothing. I was still empty, unable to decipher what I was missing.

Rather than continuing to feel sorry for myself, I opened my Pandora app and started my worship playlist I created while riding in the car with Liz. There were only eleven songs, a mixture of MercyMe, Lauren Daigle, Hillsong, and Tauren Wells. But meditating on the words helped me with establishing a sense of peace to be able to fall asleep in comfort.

On Sunday morning, I prepared for church, tucking away all the feelings and emotions I was battling the night before. Not wanting to seem out of character, I knew being in His presence would help ease the pain and help me regain the joy which was slowly slipping away.

Walking into the common area, I instantly spotted Tasha holding a conversation with a group of individuals, as she usually does. I walked over to say hello. Glad to see her glorious facial expression as we made eye contact. I smiled instantly, reaching for a much-needed hug. As I embraced her tightly, fighting back tears, she must have felt my energy because she quietly started praying, disregarding the others who were still standing there. Although I said nothing, she sensed something was wrong and stepped up as the friend she remained since the beginning, not knowing her battle with cancer indirectly stirred up emotions from my past. The fear of loss consumed me, and I was overwhelmed beyond my control.

With my eyes closed, still holding on to Tasha, I began to feel other hands touching me. Slowly I could feel them pressing on my back, one by one, until there was at least six from what I could count. Thinking it was the group of unknown individuals with whom she was speaking with earlier, it was not until Tasha's prayers became louder that I recognized the voices of the ladies from my small group standing in agreeance. They were all there, standing in my unknown battle with the word of God during the time I needed someone the most and their timing could not have been any better. Still not knowing and understanding how deeply bruised I was on the inside; it was time for me to shine some light on my situation to help them become more aware and known of what to pray for. The only way for me to become completely free was to let go of what was causing the damage, finally understanding they could give me the godly advice I needed to hear without the judgement and ridicule I was accustomed to. No longer interested in fighting the battle I was facing alone; it was time to tear down the wall and let others in.

Chapter 34

Trust, a five-letter word, yet, it holds such a powerful meaning. According to Webster, it is defined as a firm belief in the reliability, truth, ability, or strength of someone or something. But what does it look like to really trust someone? Coming into this world, our trust relies solely on our mother to provide for us, to care for us, to show us love and affection. Making it safe to say, I never understood the true meaning of trust nor how to demonstrate this with anyone else. So, what does it mean to give whole-heartedly, one hundred percent trust to God, knowing he is my sole provider and protector? He is the one going before me, and He knows my tomorrows before they happen.

In a restless generation, man may disappoint but God does not. This is something I have battled during my entire life. Too often, our expectations of others create a seatback, a feeling of emptiness or even rejection. On so many occasions I have given others the opportunity to control my actions, giving them power over my way of thinking and how I choose to view myself. I did not know the true definition of self-love nor did I understand God's love.

I began to recollect every being whom I encountered in my life, starting with my mother. My trust for her was faulty because her actions were never consistent, not even trusting herself to make better decisions. Of course, trusting my father was out of the question. He walked out on me and never looked back until I was forced into his presence for a brief amount of time. And then there was Justin. Although he proclaimed to love me, he did things behind my back to create doubt and skepticism, which caused me to lose trust for any other man who ever crossed my path. But these constant cycles of dysfunction have made the most impact on my capabilities to trust, even when it comes to trusting the One who has our best interest at heart.

I am awe-struck by these events, heartbroken, yet, learning to turn away from my own understanding. As I continue to create a closer relationship with God, I realize it was never intended for us to trust in man, no matter the status or closeness in relationship. Attempting to grasp how my life could be full of such disappointment, it was not until I started reading the scriptures that I realize trust is given to God and God only. I wanted to trust Him and to constantly reassure myself, no matter how hard the obstacles may seem, He is in full control and nothing will happen that He cannot handle.

On Monday, I attended a much-needed therapy session. Realizing it was almost two months since the last time Dr. Hunt and I met, there was a lot of catching up to do. Losing a loved one as close as Nick left my heart severely bruised and I was unsure of how to grieve, considering no one else knew the pain I was feeling. Although he was never mine to begin with, the bond we shared was one of true companions. He was there to comfort me when I needed a friend and always listened. Not too many have been able to get as close to me as he and I were, and as much as I could shine light on the negative aspects of things, I refused to allow for it to be his lasting memory.

Sitting in the lobby, I flipped through the pages of my journal that was suggested during the last visit. It was always interesting to go back and read my thoughts and how I dealt with life on certain days. It projected growth, of who I was versus who I was becoming, even for a short period of time. Some of the things I could not believe I notated on paper, but it reflected what I was feeling in those hours of discomfort. I could tell my highs from my lows, often feelings of grief and distress. Not one day went by that I did not write about Marcel. I made a mental note to reach out to him once my session was over. Although I had not spoken with him in weeks, he seemed to have been the highlight of my healing, making me happy when I would have been sad. I even wrote a few bible verses down, referencing the scripture to my pain.

"Corrie!" Dr. Hunt was standing next to the receptionist desk looking directly at me, hands on her hips, smiling from ear to ear as if she was glad to see me. I grabbed my things and followed her to the office where we always meet. Signaling for me to have a seat on the sofa next to the recliner she always sits in, she takes a sip from her coffee mug before proceeding. "So how have things been with you?"

Not knowing where to begin, I reached into my purse and pulled out my journal. "I would like to share some of my thoughts with you." I needed to show I could become more transparent and Dr. Hunt's feedback would prepare me for my next level, which was sharing with my small group. Knowing it was not something that would happen overnight, it was all a matter of trust and praying to help me get through.

Keeping my head down and eyes focused on the words in my journal, I feared making eye contact with Dr. Hunt as I began to read. My heart was pounding, and my palms were sweaty, realizing I was about to share some of my darkest moments for the first time. I flipped back to the beginning.

"Today I may be facing jail time. I don't know how I should feel about it. I'm scared, angry, and confused all in one. In a way, I expected this as the outcome for my life, but not for this reason. Maybe from being a prostitute or working in a strip club, but not for a crime I never committed. Honestly, sometimes I wish I were dead, never have been born." Right there, I paused. The thought of how blessed I was to not have went to jail intercepted everything I wrote. I began to feel an abundance of relief, reading about my yesterday, and hopeful for my tomorrows. I knew the days ahead could not be any worse than what I already experienced. Suddenly I was focused on a bigger plan for my life, realizing the worse part was now in the past and I no longer cared what others thought about me. Closing my journal, I looked up at Dr. Hunt.

"You know, I used to believe I was the victim, blaming everyone else for the things that transpired in my life. I used to think nothing good could ever happen to me and my life was cursed the day I entered this world. All these years I continued a life of destruction, sleeping with different men and not caring about the outcome. But you know what, I've found the light at the end of the road and things are getting better for me."

Seeming a little confused, Dr. Hunt was speechless. It was like I already found my resolution and her presence was no longer needed. Just having someone to talk to, someone who would give me their undivided attention and listen, made me feel a lot better. It was saying my fears aloud, so I could hear the lies and rebuttal them with truth, which made me realize it was God who delivered me from seeing jail time. It was His mercy and His grace that gave me another opportunity to get things right. Maybe the outcome of every situation would not be to my likings or satisfaction, but I was slowly learning who was in control. I needed Dr. Hunt in my life, for continued therapy and healing. But it is always God who will have the final remedy.

Chapter 35

Behold, I will do a new thing; now it shall spring forth; shall ye not know it? I will even make a way in the wilderness, and rivers in the desert.

Isaiah 43:19 KJV

My process of healing seemed to take longer than I wanted it to, but I realized, where I was at that very moment was exactly where God intended for me to be. No matter where we are in our journeys of faith, God can still use us, and he calls us right where we are.

Tuesday, only three days away from Vanessa's arrival, Tasha took me and some of the girls from small group to the shelter she spoke of at her seminar. We were going to volunteer and to participate in her ministry she started. But at our arrival and to my surprise, it was the same shelter I lived in when I first moved to Tampa, New Beginnings Women and Children Shelter. Getting out of the car, I stood in disbelief. From the outside it looked exactly how I remembered, starring at the old, worn down building as I began to piece the puzzles together, realizing Tasha had known of me the entire time. She knew where to find me at the club and became eager for me to let her in but the only way of doing that was to become more like me to get my attention. Never did I imagine stepping foot back on this ground, not wanting to look back to the place it all started. Tears began to swell up and I could not hold back the emotions I was feeling. I was facing fear right in its face and could no longer hide from the truth of my past. Unable to manipulate my circumstances any longer, I refused to remain defeated and destroyed.

I looked around to notice all attention on me and Tasha walking towards my direction. Extending her arms out, she whispered, "I'm here for you", as she embraced me tightly. I began to vaguely remember seeing her around whenever I was there, but I never gave it a second thought. Realizing this was the closure I was seeking as part of my healing process; I could not fault her for bringing me to this point. I began to understand the role she was destined to play in my life and how God knew this would all happen. His timing…His will…His purpose in order to renew, rebuild, and restore.

I wanted to go inside, look around, and see the place where I once laid my head, realizing how much of a difference life was for me years later. No longer a slave to my past, the shackles were coming off and chains were being broken. I no longer possessed the same thought process I arrived in Tampa with, nor was I bound to the same destructive behavior. My walk was different, my talk was different, and I knew who I belonged to.

We all walked in together, step by step, Tasha leading the way through the entrance. Seeing the open space with all the beds lined up, side by side, brought back so many memories, looking upon so many faces filled with hope and determination. I wanted to help and become a part of giving back to the shelter that once opened its doors to a lost soul like myself. Having plenty of money in the bank from the sale of my building, I wanted to do something positive with those earnings and not just spend them on useless belongings I did not really need. Making a mental note, I decided to wait and come back without the other ladies.

We spent the rest of the day huddled in groups, praying for and with the women and children. Listening to so many different stories from each of the families, they were no different from my own. We all could relate to one another and no one was there to judge. I was still in my early stages of trusting God and learning how to take my place in His story, rather than my own. Realizing I was no longer living for the things I desired, I could not construct my life with my own strength. I was not equipped with the ability to do so. Yet, these were the lies I once believed. When one of the ladies asked me if I used to live in the same shelter she was now living in, I replied without hesitation, "yes, in that bed right over there", pointing to the right from where we were sitting, at a bed that appeared to be unoccupied. I could remember laying there wondering how long I would be confined to just this space, overwhelmed by the life I was born into and mad at my parents for allowing such turmoil to have existed. Forgiveness in my heart allowed me to lay down that pain, at the cross, where I left it once and for all. I was no longer bitter, angry and upset for the things in which were out of my control and I could feel my growth as I was becoming less of myself. My joy was not found when I was fighting and reaching for comfort. It was all within my pain, giving me a reason to reach for Christ. I was learning how to connect relationally, showing love and mercy to others. No longer wondering about the future, it was all about the right now. I recognized Tasha's discipleship as an attempt to reach the loss, such as myself and every moment was leading up to an invitation to allow her inside my world. She desperately desired a deeper understanding and I became more eager to let her in.

We formed a circle, approximately twelve ladies, Tasha, Liz, Courtney and I included. Amber led a separate group, along with Tracie, in a different area. As we gathered, I realized it was our desire for a closer relationship with God that brought us all together yet our similarities in circumstances that allowed us to show compassion towards one another. Nothing was by coincidence. It was all part of God's timing.

Tasha led the group in prayer before beginning her actual discussion on a topic which hit close to home, rejection, a subject we all related closely to. Whether from our past or our present, the torment of rejection played a role in all our lives at one point or another and my life was a perfect example. She continued by referencing two specific bible verses; Isaiah 41:9, which reads, ***Thou whom I have taken from the ends of the earth, and called thee from the chief men thereof, and said unto thee Thou art my servant; I have chosen thee, and not cast thee away.***, and Psalms 27:10, ***When my father and my mother forsake me, then the Lord will take me up.*** She paused briefly, looking around the circle in silence as we all sat motionless, taking in each scripture and its meaning. My progress allowed me to understand how they both related to my past transgressions and I wanted to be the first to elaborate on the topic a little deeper.

"I was rejected by both of my parents." I started to speak as all eyes began to focus in my direction. My palms began to become sweaty while nervousness was setting in, but I knew it was my time to become transparent about what I had been through. Taking a deep breath, I continued, reminiscing as if it were just yesterday. "My mom committed suicide when I was young. I guess life was too much for here to withstand. And my dad was never available, not even when I was forced to live with him for a few years. I thought nobody loved me, so I went looking for it in all the wrong places, doing things I am not proud of. I was young, naïve, and full of this world."

Hearing myself speak and admitting my transgressions aloud, made me realize how proud I was of the woman I was becoming. I recognized the growth while learning we all battle a sinful nature because of the world we are born into. It required much time and effort to be conformed to the image of Christ, as I began to fall more in love with the idea of submitting only to Him.

"Moving to Tampa, I was in survival mode, attempting to create a life outside of what God intended for me to have. Starting at this shelter, there was no family, and no money, just a determination to make a name for myself. I didn't know God at that time. Although I had not consciously rejected Him, I lacked understanding to who was in control. Living day to day with no purpose or meaning, I was going through the motions, resulting in stripping and prostitution."

Speculations of judgement invaded my thoughts briefly at my last statement, assuming the worse. But the fear soon subsided as I noticed the ladies looking at me with sympathy and understanding. I was getting a taste of true freedom, no longer a slave to my sins nor embarrassed of what others would think of me if they found out about my past. In my search for a new way of living I was finding peace, healing, and forgiveness of myself. Yes, I'll say that again… FORGIVENESS OF MYSELF. As reluctant as I became to admit my shame to others, it was truly myself who I was afraid of. I did not want to admit I lacked true forgiveness in my heart of all the things I engaged in, both knowing and unknowing, that were wrong and disgraceful to the person whom God called me to be. I learned, concealing my secrets only caused more damage because I was unable to let go and was constantly reminded of my sins. The deliverance of my testimony was a perfect way to minister to other people and move past the biggest obstacle I was facing.

A few other women spoke once I was done and then Tasha ended in prayer before concluding our session for the day. The few who were from my small group ministry walked over to give me a hug, including Tasha, letting me know how proud they were of my progress. I wanted it to continue, knowing I still needed to face Vanessa, the one whom I owed an explanation to. As her parent, it was my duty to share my past experiences with her. And all I could do was pray for her acceptance.

That night when I arrived home, I received a phone call from Justin, informing me of his flight on Thursday morning, the day before Vanessa was scheduled to arrive. Not having anything else planned, I told him I could pick him up from the airport, eager to find out as much information as I could possibly stand about the daughter whom I did not know. But once disconnecting the call, I began to question how my dad was feeling before my arrival to New York. How did he react when social services informed him of the turn of events that transpired? It was the same circumstances, realizing my behaviors were the same of my parents. He chose to not be a part of my life just as I chose to walk away from Vanessa's. Yet, it was life's episodes that forced me back into his presence. So, what occurrence allowed me a second chance? Afterall, nothing happens by coincidence.

Chapter 36

On Wednesday morning I was up at the break of dawn, anxious for the events that were taking place on the days to follow, I could no longer sleep. Reflecting on all that transpired on yesterday, I was convinced my mind was being renewed, giving God permission to completely reconstruct my perspective of thinking. I began to take inventory of my soul. What things did I need to correct? To whom did I owe an apology? What did I need to let go of?

Sliding out of bed, I decided there was some unfinished business I needed to attend to. While getting dressed in my all grey sweat suit, I sent out a text to a person I needed to apologize to the most. Hoping she would find room in her heart for forgiveness and to allow me closure I was so desperately seeking, I began to pray as I hit the send button. I sat the phone down on the bed, beside me, as I put on my socks and tennis shoes. With every minute that went by, I could not help but feel as though I was being ignored. But as soon as the doubts began to overwhelm me, my phone buzzed with a returned text, a message that read, see you in a few.

I grabbed my purse and keys, contemplating how the conversation would play out in my head. Aside from anything else, I knew I needed to humble myself, with an understanding that anything said was coming from a place of pain and should not be taken out of context. I was ready for this chapter of my life to be closed once and for all, to forgive myself and receive healing. Searching for peace and realizing it cannot be found in the things on this earth nor through other people, I was slowly growing in my own faith. It is God's desire for us to all feel peace, joy and a feeling of purpose. Although the peace of God is not always something that we can figure out for ourselves, it is available to us and extended to every person who accepts Jesus as their savior.

Pulling into the Oaklawn Cemetery, I drove around until locating Leslie's car. I parked and took a deep breath before getting out and joining her at Nick's grave site. My first time ever visiting, I was overwhelmed with emotions, attempting to fight back tears as we made eye contact. From her expression, I knew she had been crying, which triggered my emotions as I began to break down as well. Pausing in my path, Leslie walked over to console me, embracing me with a huge hug. We cried together, equally understanding how important this encounter was for the both of us. Once regaining my composure, I held on to her a little longer, continuing to be a shoulder for her to cry on.

"Leslie I am so sorry", I began to genuinely apologize as we were letting go. "I pray you can find forgiveness in your heart and understand how I never intentionally meant to hurt you. I was broken. I was lost. I was in such a dark place." Beginning to cry once more, I was not only confessing to Leslie, but surrendering myself to God, allowing Him full control. Hurt people, hurt people and I no longer desired to be a part of the cycle and the work of the enemy. My participation in tearing down a marriage created chaos in so many lives, including my own, not realizing how I was contributing to my own self-destruction. At the end, I was hurting myself more than anyone else, desiring something that did not belong to me and bowing down to my own sexual desires, desires of the flesh, which only led to death. My soul was dying as I was suffocating, starving, and dehydrated. But despite all I been through, it was by God's grace, I was able to be cleansed, renewed, and given a fresh start.

"Corrie, thank you so much for your kind words. I forgive you and I continue to pray for you daily. I'm in a better place now and I could not be more at peace. I loved my husband but you and I both knew his lifestyle would catch up with him sooner than later. I tried to tell him to stop but he always desired more. He was empty and did not understand how the things of this world would soon fade away. I just pray God has mercy on his soul and that, amid the torture and pain he experienced during his last days, he was able to repent and ask God for forgiveness. It wasn't your fault and nothing you could have done would have stopped what God already planned for his life. He calls out to all His children, but we are given the decision to respond to that calling or continue our path. Nick chose his."

Looking me directly in the eyes with contentment, she gave me a half smile. "I'll let you say your goodbyes a little longer, as I have other engagements to attend to. But thanks again and may God continue to do His great works through you." And with nothing left to be said, she smiled and walked towards her car.

Taking a few more minutes, I stared at Nick's headstone, feeling like his premature death contributed to my salvation and deliverance. "Goodbye Nick", I mumbled, turning away and walking towards the parking lot, realizing I would never need to revisit this space again in my life. In time the pain would fade, and the memories would be just that, memories of a chapter I was gracefully able to walk away from. With my chin up, I started the car and drove away, blasting Zoe Worship music, Momentum.

On the ride home I received a phone call I anticipated for days. It was Liz's mother calling to invite me to interview with the Board of Directors for the instructor position. She mentioned hearing nothing but great things about me and thought I would be a great fit for the job. Attempting to maintain my composure, I accepted with no hesitation, halfway in tears as I could feel God moving through my life and the shift that was taking place. He was opening doors and clearing my path, guiding me into my destiny. This did not mean the battle was over. It only meant I was developing a better understanding of the One who was in full control. I was learning that, no matter what trials I face, I was not alone. Through all the rejection, He was there. Through the loss of loved ones, He was there. Through my sexual abuse, He was there. Even when I was ready to give up on myself, He has been there all along, patiently waiting for me to hear His voice and respond with love, forgiveness, and mercy. No longer a slave to my past, I was equipped with the armor I needed to face each day with confidence and determination. Eager to share the great news, I could not wait to attend small group that night so I could tell the ladies about my upcoming interview.

Chapter 37

I was more nervous than I had ever been in my entire life when Thursday finally came around. Preparing to see Justin for the first time after so many years, I did not know what to say nor how to respond. Do I hug him, shake his hand, knell down and pray for his deliverance, so many thoughts were running through my head? So much changed over the past fourteen years, and yet, I was beginning to discredit my progress by reliving past mistakes. The only thing I could think to do was put on some worship music and clean my house from top to bottom, not expecting his plane to land for at least two more hours.

Still remembering our last encounter as if it were yesterday, I remember Vanessa and I spending the entire afternoon in Jersey with Justin and his parents, shopping and enjoying the scenery. Everyone seemed to be in a happy space, laughing and enjoying the moment, except for me. I was miserable and suffering from postpartum depression, desperately wanting my old life back. By that time, Justin found out about my real age because I was trying to juggle school and take care of an infant. Once I told him I was pregnant, he insisted on becoming a family. But I had other plans on my agenda that did not include being tied down to responsibilities. For days, I searched for a way out, but I was too young to fathom the consequences that were involved.

Interrupting my thoughts, the alarm I set for myself was buzzing, as an indication of only having an hour to get to the airport. Grabbing my belongings, I took another glance over the house before turning off the lights and walking out the door. The time had arrived, and it was really happening. The only thing I could do was pray and exhale, driving towards downtown Tampa in silence. I realized how much changed in fourteen years and wondered if Justin even looked the same.

Sitting impatiently in my car, I watched as people walked in and out of the sliding doors, anticipating Justin to be one of them. The seconds felt like minutes and minutes were more like dragging, workday hours. As my nervousness began to overtake my body, my stomach began to bubble, and I immediately got the urge to go to the bathroom. Not now, I thought to myself. Parked in the express lane, I could not leave my car sitting with the expectation of it not being towed before I returned. I realized my only option was to park in the parking garage and go inside the airport to use the restroom. Taking out my phone, I attempted to call Justin to get his location, but it went straight to voicemail. Maybe his flight was delayed, and he was still in the air, giving enough time to relieve myself and be back in the car before he would realize I was missing in action.

Hurriedly walking through the airport, I eluded large crowds and people walking with luggage. My focus was getting to the bathroom and getting back to the car before Justin would call. As I rushed into the ladies' room, my attitude shifted, noticing a line of other women waiting to get into a stall. Still being mindful of the time, the line moved faster than expected and I was out of there within enough minutes before Justin started calling.

"Where you at?", Justin was asking on the other end of the phone. "I am walking through the airport, back to the parking garage."

"Well, I am grabbing my luggage from baggage claim. Want to grab some lunch while we're both inside?" Not expecting to hang out in the airport, I hesitantly answered, "sure, but there aren't many options to choose from." I really wanted to get to a more quiet, secluded place so we could talk about Vanessa before her arrival, which was less than twenty-four hours away. There was so much information to cram in within such little time.

"How about we stop at a restaurant on the way out?", I suggested, hoping he would accept my invitation.

"Yeah that will be fine, but since you are already inside, why don't you just meet me in baggage claim, so I won't have to look for you afterwards." Before I was able to object, he hung up the phone, refusing to take no for an answer. Turning from my planned course, I began to walk towards the other side to meet him, thinking it would not be so bad. It was beginning to feel like a blind date, only, we had history and a child together. Walking through the airport in my grey, linear joggers, my white slim-fit tank top, and all black air force ones, I realized I was dressed the same as I used to back in the day when we would hang out.

"Corrie!", I heard a masculine voice, with a New York accent yell my name and immediately knew it was him. Turning around, he walked over and embraced me tighter than I ever been hugged before. With my arms around his neck, I held on for minutes, inhaling his cologne while holding back emotions. I was happy to be in his presence, finally knowing he was safe and well. Minutes went by before he let go, and when he did, I noticed tears drawing up in his eyes.

"Are you crying?", I asked jokingly. And looking down at me like he always did, we both just smiled, expecting it to be an emotional occasion after being apart for so many years.

"So, what do you have a taste for? You want some pizza?"

"Nah, I don't want pizza from down south." He laughed, knowing I would not take offense to his comment, while beginning to miss the taste of a real, brick oven, New York style pizza. Smiling from ear to ear, I felt nothing but joy, glad to have him in the city with me for the time being.

Walking to the car, our conversation was as though we never lost touch and I was excited to have someone from my past finally come see me for once. We drove to a restaurant not far from our location and on the way there we laughed and joked about old times, talked about the difference in the weather, and even about the events that took place on his flight, which explained the delay. But never once did he bring up Vanessa. Wanting to be the one to break the ice, I thought it would be more comfortable for me to bring it up and control the conversation once being seated at our table.

The Hard Rock Café was my place of choice, considering they would have enough variety for Justin's picky taste. We both ordered water while taking time to look over the menu.

"How long are you staying?", asking the first question, leading up to the information I was really wanting to know. "That all depends on how well Vanessa adjust to being here." Justin lowered the menu so we could look one another eye to eye.

"Co, Vanessa knows more than you think she does. My reason for visiting is to make sure you…are ready for this transition."

Unsure of what he meant, I began to dig deeper into what he knew and what I was not being told. For years, my only recollection of my daughter was of the flowers she sent me every year. Although never questioning how she knew where I was, there must have been some sort of conversation between here and her father, which created a deeper understanding of myself and the situation.

"I'm going to tell you something and I don't want you to be upset. Which, I really don't see how you could, considering every decision I made for Vanessa was for her wellbeing, but I need to make sure you are in the right mentality to accept what I am about to say." Interrupted by the waitress, we quickly gave her our orders, hurriedly rushing her away to continue our discussion. I was eager to hear what he was about to say, feeling nothing could break me from the space I was in and the peace I was feeling.

"Vanessa knows who you are, and she is excited to start a life with you. For the past two years she has been preparing herself for this moment, hoping you would be as accepting of her as she is of you."

Still not understanding where all of this was going, I was becoming impatient and wanted him to get to the point. How did she know about me if I was not there? What did Justin tell her? Remembering she was only eleven months when I walked away, there was no traces of me left behind.

"She grew up with your dad and Dana."

And there it was. Justin blurted out the words he knew I would not be so eager to hear. They would shut me down in my tracks and leave me feeling empty and questioning the outcome of every encounter. I could remember how angry my dad was when I told him I was pregnant. I could still hear his voice, begging me to have an abortion. So, trying to understand the logics of the entire situation just did not make sense to me.

"Not too long after you moved to Tampa, Dana reached out to me, said she wanted to see Vanessa and asked if I could bring her over. I wasn't going to deny my child the opportunity to get to know her grandparents based off your upbringing. Everyone deserves a second chance Co." He was attempting to convince me with reasoning. But there were no objections from my end. "When I saw the look on your dad's face, holding her, it was like he was regretting not being there for you. I could see where he realized he messed up and it was like getting a second chance."

Feeling deep gratitude, I was happy my daughter experienced true love and adoration like I never felt before. Through her, I felt like my dad's memories lived on and there was so much she could tell me about him. Finding out throughout the conversation with Justin that she spent most of the time with them before their passing, she made him promise to bring her to me once she would be old enough, desiring a life with having a mother. She was already prepared for rejection and disappointment but filled with joy when finding out I wanted her just as much as she wanted me. My heart was full, crying tears of joy because I no longer held on to bitterness towards my father and I knew I could visit at any time because Justin and Vanessa knew exactly where he was buried.

We ate our food as we continued to discuss the gaps in the last fourteen years, me telling him everything that took place in my life thus far, leaving out no details. Justin was the only one who knew everything about my past, other than me telling Marcel of the things he needed to know to win my case, Justin was my day one best friend who always had my back throughout the toughest of times. I knew he would not judge me, even when I could not explain some things. He understood my brokenness and wanted me to, 'be good to myself', as he would always tell me. So, when he discovered I turned my life around and how I was now saved, he felt honored that I would invite him to join me for church on Sunday morning.

Chapter 38

Thy hands have made me and fashioned me: give me understanding, that I may learn thy commandments. They that fear thee will be glad when they see me; because I have hoped in thy word.

Psalms 119:73-74 KJV

God is not trying to fix us; He wants to heal us. Every event leading up to Vanessa's arrival was all in His plan and intended to make me stronger. It all began to make sense as I revisited the shelter I once lived and reconnecting with Justin to fill in the pieces I was once missing. Maybe it was my stubbornness that allowed me to stay blinded for so long. But now the darkness was gone, and I was walking with a much better vision.

The next morning when I awakened, I could hear laughter coming from the other room, the voice of Justin and a young girl, knowing exactly who's it was. I looked at the clock, not realizing how late I slept. Jumping out of bed, I put on my slippers and rushed into the other room, finding Vanessa and Justin in the kitchen cooking breakfast. I stood in disbelief, my heart full of joy and eyes full of tears. The moment finally arrived, and I was speechless. When she turned around to realize I was standing behind her, she leaped into my arms and hugged me so tightly, not wanting to let go. All I could do was cry. Thank you, God, was all I could think in my head, as flashbacks of holding my baby girl for the first time appeared. I felt restored, given a second chance to live life according to God's purpose. Nothing could take away the joy I was feeling on the outside, and the peace I finally found within.

She was so beautiful, with big brown eyes, long, wavy hair, and radiant, brown skin just like her mother. It was almost like looking at myself when I was her age. I wanted to know everything about her. What was her favorite color, food, things to do in her spare time? What made her laugh, what made her cry, and all of life's experiences up until that point? Getting to know Vanessa was going to be a journey I was ready to embrace.

"When did you get here?", I asked as we walked over to take a seat on the sofa.

"About an hour ago", she answered in a soft, innocent tone. "Daddy came to pick me up from the airport and we got to ride in an Uber." She giggled with excitement and we both began to laugh. It was the most happiness I experienced since I could remember, and her presence gave me life. I stared at her, admiring her child like demeanor and realizing she was nothing like I was at her age. I must have thanked God at least a dozen times just in that moment, still seeming surreal and unbelievable.

"Would you like to see your room?", I asked, looking over at the luggage sitting in the corner. I was excited for my effort of creating an amazing, girly space. Decorated with rainbow colors and unicorns, I found the idea on Pinterest and thought she would love it. But the glow on her face was more than I could have ever imagined. Looking around like it was something she had never seen before, I stood in the doorway as she admired all her belongings.

   Justin walked up behind me, eager to peek at the space as well. "Who'd you hire to do this?" As he pushed past me to join Vanessa on her tour.

"I actually did this by myself. Do you like it?"

"Yes, I love it!", Vanessa exclaimed while Justin just winked his eye at me with approval. It was confirmation that I was ready to embark on the journey ahead. Vanessa walked over to her bag, pulled out a picture frame, and placed it on her nightstand next to her bed. It was a picture of my dad holding her up in the air. From the looks of her size, she had to be no older than two, maybe three.

"That's your grandpa." Not wanting her to know the pain I was feeling inside, I walked over to get a closer look.

"Yep", she answered, watching my reaction like she already knew how I was going to respond. "He loved you very much mama." She continued to plead his case, yet, not understanding the extent of pain I once experienced. Not being able to say goodbye nor that I was sorry, tormented my thoughts every night. And although I tried to shift my thinking to something more positive, the guilt still bothered my soul.

"I loved him too Vanessa. But it was just different." I wanted to share my own experiences with her so that she too could have a better understanding of my life and how God can change anyone. Although my relationship with my father was entirely different from what she once experienced, she could never fully understand the things I once endured. Having grandkids was like a do over of the mistakes they made as parents, learning a little more patience and understanding. I loved my dad and I missed out on the opportunity to make things right with him. But I was not going to allow that to be my story with my own child. God makes no mistakes and His timing could not have been more perfect. Unable to live my life in regret, though deeply saddened, I knew I was delivered. There were several things that remained true to my life and all of our lives, God is not surprised by any of the actions taken against us, He was in full control and allowed everything to happen for His purpose and as part of His plan, and His word promises He would never leave nor forsake any of us. My stories, my journey, and all my pain was now a testimony for others.

Chapter 39

The things I have learned throughout every situation… pain, anger, disappointment, grief… they are all temporary. It is easy to cry about what we do not have, rather than applying effort to become more thankful for the things we do, as well as the circumstances we are delivered from along the way. If you don't allow correction, you will remain foolish and, in the darkness, as doubt, depression, and confusion consume your thoughts.

After all that transpired, I no longer desired to live life according to the way that would please others. Instead, my focus became more on things eternal and less of the right now's. I understood how life on earth was temporary, and we all had to serve a purpose. I also understood how we should enjoy those who love us while they are still here, appreciating loyalty and fellowship. Evolving into the person whom God intended for me to be, over time I could see how we put too much emphasis on the appearance of the outside rather than reconstructing what is inside. It is about love, kindness, patience, generosity, and forgiveness; treating others the way we would want to be treated.

On Sunday, Justin, Vanessa and I attended church and I was able to share one of the most powerful, life changing experiences with the people who cared the most. I made the decision to be baptized. Submerged in water and coming up feeling restored, there was no turning back and I was thankful for another chance at life. I had been delivered from my bad habits and selfishness, redirecting my path to what is good.

Enjoying time spent with my daughter meant more to me than anything I thought I desired. I realized how much material possessions only left me empty, alone, and wanting more, but once I received a taste of true, abundant life, nothing else mattered. We enjoyed the rest of the summer, time spent getting to know one another on a more personal level. I was able to reveal to her the truth about my life, with the help of Dr. Hunt, who sat with us regularly. And her forgiveness meant more to me than words could ever describe. I was finally able to introduce her to Tasha and my other newly found friends from my small group, who accepted and loved her like their own.

Tasha has still been ministering to the lost and broken, disregarding her circumstances, in order to speak life into others. My admiration grows more and more for her daily, as I watch lives being changed and relationships being restored. She is constantly searching for women to reach through her own testimony, giving them hope and teaching them a better way. And even now, in her stage four of cancer, she still prays for God to allow her to reach just one more.

Justin eventually went back to New York but is a frequent visitor of Florida, giving us the opportunity to get to know one another from a new, more understanding level. Turns out, nothing was wrong with him and he was only trying to create a bond between a broken mother and hurting daughter, a change that was necessary for healing. I never realized, when I met him as a young girl, the important role he would play now that I am older.

Marcel moved on with his life, never looking back once he returned to Atlanta. I attempted to reach out on several occasions, but I could never get an answer, considering his time in my life was no longer necessary and accepting the short role he played in it. He was only there to help me in my time of trouble, sent by God to pull me out of the mess I was so deeply in, so I could find the rest I was seeking. And although he sporadically crossed my mind, I am at peace with how things turned out.

As for myself, my job interview went well and I am now a full time, massage therapy instructor. Giving up everything I thought I needed to hold on to, allowed for me to receive the things that were intended for me to have. Of course, there were times when doubt tried to creep in, but in those times, I prayed harder, I worshipped louder, and I read my bible even longer. Still attending small group regularly, my support system was strong, having friends who were standing in agreement with prayer whenever I was too weak to face my fears alone. I was learning how to put on the full armor of God and trust in Him through every circumstance. Nobody told me this journey would be easy, but just a little faith and a person who cares can go a long way.

If ye then be risen with Christ, seek those things which are above, where Christ sitteth on the right hand of God.

Set your affection on things above, not on things on the earth.

For ye are dead, and your life is hid with Christ in God.

When Christ, who is our life, shall appear, then shall ye also appear with Him in glory.

Colossians 3:1-4 KJV

Acknowledgements

To thank and acknowledge everyone who have played a significant role in my life would be a book in itself, however, what is understood should never have to be explained, and it is only through actions that I could ever show my deepest love and appreciation to all. Humbly, fighting back tears as I write, I thank God for the continuous, never wavering presence of all my immediate family, friends and loved ones.

To my Heavenly Father, my Savior, my guide through the darkest times, I am so thankful for the sacrifices You made just for me. Thank You for never giving up on me and for Your grace and mercy that You give so generously. It is through You that I have been made brave and bold. It is in Your power that I can view life through a different lens. God, I pray that You continue to fill me with your presence, with Your peace, and comfort. I only desire the life You have for me because I know it is good!

To my nurturer, disciplinarian, fuss box, bailout plan, my EVERYTHING, I could not imagine these thirty-six years without you in them. God sought you fit to carry out His plan of being my mother and through all the ups and downs we have faced, you have always had my back, front, and both sides. Your strength and work ethic have taught me to push through every circumstance, never giving up on my dreams and aspirations. Thank you for your guidance and unconditional love throughout the years. As a single mother, I salute you for your determination, your sacrifice for your children even when it meant not having for yourself, and for your courage to admit when you did not have all the answers. I love you mommy!

Jomo, my brother and very first nuisance in life, I need you to know that your move to the west coast has created a reason for me to miss you, as well as an appreciation to be your little sister. No matter how many times I told you I disliked you when we were growing up and how complicated you made it for me to be the youngest, I would not trade you for anyone else in the world. All your grammar corrections, which I am sure even now you have critiqued every detail of my writing, and your attempts to beat me with your tennis rackets, have contributed to the woman I have become today. (LOL) No matter how far apart we may live from one another, nothing could ever extinguish the constant love I have for you. I love you and pray nothing but amazing things to happen in your life.

To my heartbeats, Kiera and Kayla, I LOVE YOU! I LOVE YOU! I LOVE YOU! Never stop pushing! Never stop fighting! Never stop being YOU! There are going to be so many disappointments throughout your lifetime but remember the One who goes before you, clearing your path and preparing you for His plan. Remember He is faithful, He is constant, and He is the best friend you will ever have…PERIOD! Never allow anyone to change who you are nor allow them to bring you out of your character. And throughout every disappointment, failure, and heartache, remember to love, show mercy, and to forgive.

Danielle, my best friend, sister from another mister, my secret keeper… from childhood to adulthood, you have been in my corner every step of the way, cheering me on to the finish line in every circumstance. We have laughed, cried, celebrated, and experienced many disagreements, yet, through it all, your friendship has remained constant. Thank you for your patience with me and for your support throughout writing this book. You have become one of my biggest cheerleaders, helping me to remain focused when I was ready to give up. I love you and we are going to ride this thang until the rims fall off!

Jessica, my spiritual sister in Christ, surely you did not think I could write acknowledgements without acknowledging the one who contributed to leading me to true salvation. When I was in my darkest place, you were there. When I had no one else to turn to, in a city where family was nonexistent, you were there. It is because of you that I have found true peace. I am a firm believer that God places people in your life at the right time, and you are one of those people who I have been blessed to encounter. Any friend who leads you to the house of the Lord, is a friend worth hanging on to. I admire your faith and I thank you for all the encouragements, the hospitality you have shown me and my daughters throughout the years, and for being the ear when I need to rant about life's circumstances. I can't wait to see what God has in store for you. I love you girl!

To Candace Johnson, Ryan Shaw, and Jessie Jensen, thank you guys so much for being such a huge part of this book. Your creativity and eye for art is a blessing from God and I am so thankful to have the opportunity to utilize your services. Thank you for taking time out of your busy schedules to make my dream come to life. You took my vision and perfected it beyond my expectations. Your fragments of experiences have collectively been a great inspiration to me being able to complete this project and I am so excited to see where He leads you in your career and endeavors.

May God continue to bless all of you!

Made in the USA
Columbia, SC
10 July 2023